Books by Harry Crews

A Feast of Snakes

Harry Crews

New York

A Feast of Snakes

ATHENEUM

Atheneum
Macmillan Publishing Company
866 Third Avenue, New York, NY 10022
Collier Macmillan Canada, Inc.

Library of Congress Cataloging in Publication Data

Crews, Harry, 1935–
  A feast of snakes.

  I. Title.
PZ4.C9175Fe   [PS3553.R46]   813'.5'4   76-8206
ISBN 0-689-10729-3
Paperback:
ISBN 0-689-70715-0   LCCN 86-47945

Lines from "If I Could Only Live at the Pitch That Is Near Madness" are quoted from *Collected Poems* by Richard Eberhart, published by Oxford University Press and used by permission.

10   9

Printed in the United States of America

This book is for **Johnny Feiber:** *in good times and bad I've never raised a glass with a better friend.*

If I could only live at the pitch that is near madness
When everything is as it was in my childhood
Violent, vivid, and of infinite possibility:
That the sun and moon broke over my head.

Richard Eberhart

Part One

She felt the snake between her breasts, felt him there, and loved him there, coiled, the deep tumescent S held rigid, ready to strike. She loved the way the snake looked sewn onto her V-neck letter sweater, his hard diamondback pattern shining in the sun. It was unseasonably hot, almost sixty degrees, for early November in Mystic, Georgia, and she could smell the light musk of her own sweat. She liked the sweat, liked the way it felt, slick as oil, in all the joints of her body, her bones, in the firm sliding muscles, tensed and locked now, ready to spring—to *strike* —when the band behind her fired up the school song: "Fight On Deadly Rattlers of Old Mystic High."

She felt a single drop of sweat slip from the small of her back, hang for an instant, and then slide into the mellow groove between the flexed jaws of her ass. When she felt the sweat touch her there, she automatically cut her eyes to see if she could pick out Willard Miller, the Boss Snake of all the Mystic Rattlers, *her* boss Snake, pick him out from the other helmeted and white-suited boys scrimmaging on the other side of the track. When they made contact, their soft, almost gentle grunts came to her across the green practice field.

She tried to distinguish the sound of him from the sound of the others, and she thought she could, thought how amazingly the sound was like the ragged snorts he made into her ear when he had her bent brutally back over the hood of her Vette. There was hardly any difference at all in the noise he made when he scored on the field or scored on her. In whatever he did, he was always noisy and violent and wet, tending as he did to slobber a little.

She saw the band director raise his baton and she tensed, rolled her weight forward to the balls of her feet, and then the music was crashing around her, the tubas pumping, the drums rattling, and she was strutting like it was the end of the world. From the sides of the field came the dry, awesome rattle of the diamondback. Some of the fans had come out and they had brought their gourds with them. The gourds were as big as cantaloupes, shaped like crooked-neck squash, and full of dried seed so that when they were shaken they vibrated the air with the genuine sound of a snake. During a game, the home stands of the Mystic Rattlers put everybody's hair on end. You could hear those dried gourd seeds two miles away, buzzing like the biggest snake den God ever imagined. During football season, nobody in Mystic was very far from his gourd. Sometimes you could see people carrying them around with them in town, down at the grocery store, or inside Simpkin's, the only dry goods store in Mystic.

The band was strung out now in the shape of a snake. The band members used the yard markers to position themselves, double timing in place, drawing their knees high and waving their instruments, so that the entire snake vibrated in the sun. The snare drums were under one goal post, rattling for all they were worth and she was under the other goal post, standing in the snake's mouth, her arms rigid as fangs. She was at one with the music. She did not have to think to perform. Of all the majorettes—and there were five others —she marched in place with the highest knees, the biggest smile, the finest skin, the best teeth. She was a natural, and as a natural her one flaw—if she had one—was that her mind tended to wander. She didn't have to think, didn't have to concentrate like the other girls to get her moves right. Consequently she sometimes got bored with the drills and her mind wandered. Even now as she pranced in place, her back arched, her pelvis thrust forward, she was winking at Joe Lon Mackey where he stood under the end zone bleachers.

That was where he usually stood when he watched them practice and she was not surprised to see him there, glad rather, because it gave her something to think about. He wasn't twenty feet from her, standing in the shadows, a burlap sack in one hand and a brown paper sipping sack in the other. From time to time he raised the sipping sack to his mouth. He'd winked at her when she first stopped under the goal post. She'd winked back. Turned her smile on him. She'd always liked him. Hell, *everybody* had always liked Joe Lon. But she didn't really know him *that* well. Her sister, who was going to school at the University of Georgia in Athens, her sister, Berenice, knew him *that* well.

Her sister and Joe Lon had been a number in Mystic, Georgia, in all of Lebeau County for that matter, and Joe Lon could have been going to the University of Georgia in Athens or anywhere else in this country he wanted to except it turned out Joe Lon was not a good student. That's the way they all put it there in Mystic: Joe Lon Mackey is not a good student. But it was worse than that and they all knew it. It had never been established exactly if Joe Lon could read. Most of the teachers at Mystic High who had been privileged to have him in their classrooms thought he probably couldn't. But they liked him anyway, even loved

him, loved tall, blond, high school All-American Joe Lon
Mackey whose exceptional quietness off the playing field
everybody chose to call courtesy. He had the name of being
the most courteous boy in all of Lebeau County, although
it was commonly known that he had done several pretty bad
things, one of which was taking a traveling salesman out to
July Creek and drowning him while nearly the entire first
string watched from high up on the bank where they were
sipping beer.

She missed the band director's whistle signaling that the
snake was about to strike and consequently the five other
girls making up the snake's head almost knocked her over.
She'd been standing, her arms positioned as fangs, winking
at Joe Lon where he raised his sack in the shadows and
wondering if Berenice would come home for the roundup,
when the girl right behind her, highstepping, hit her in the
kidney with a knee and almost knocked her down. She
caught herself just in time and hissed over her shoulder:
"You want you ass kicked, do you?"

The girl said something back to her but it was lost in the
pumping tubas. Under the stands Joe Lon Mackey took the
last pull from a Jim Beam half pint and dropped the paper
sack with the bottle in it into the weeds. He took out two
pieces of Dentyne chewing gum and put them into his mouth.
Then he lit a cigarette. He had been watching Candy—
called Hard Candy by nearly everybody but her parents,
Dr. and Mrs. Sweet—because she reminded him of Berenice
and all the things that might have come true for him but
had not. Two years ago Berenice had been a senior and
head majorette and he, Joe Lon, had been Boss Rattler.

It was said that Joe Lon, on any given day of his senior
year of high school, could have run through the best college
defensive line in the country. But he had not. He had never
set foot on a single college football field even though he had

been invited to visit more than fifty colleges and universities. But that was all right. He'd had his. That's what he told himself about ten times a day: *That's all right. By God, I had mine.*

He reached into the back pocket of his Levis and pulled out a sheet of blue paper. It was almost worn through in the creases where it was folded. He shook it open and held it up to the light. It said: "I will see you at rattlesnake time. Love Berenice." There were some X's under the name. The letter had come to Joe Lon at the store three days ago. It had taken him most of the afternoon to be sure of the words and once he was sure of them, they had given him no pleasure. He had thought he was through with all that, had made his peace. He folded the letter and put it back in his pocket. But on the way to his pickup he took the letter out again and, using his teeth and his free hand, he carefully tore it into very small pieces and left them scattered behind him in the gloomy aisle underneath the stands.

He drove over to the little road that went by the practice field and watched Willard Miller run the ball. They were running him against the grunions, the smaller, second-string boys who came out for football for God knows what reason since they almost never got into a game and could only offer up their bodies as tackling dummies for the bigger, stronger boys. He watched Willard Miller fire three straight times up the middle. It was important to run him against grunions now and then. It gave him a chance to practice his moves without running the risk of getting injured. It also gave him great opportunities to run over people and step on them, mash their heads and their hands, kick their ribs good.

Joe Lon felt his own thigh muscles tick, as he watched Willard fake a grunion out of his shoes and then, after he had the boy entirely turned around and beaten, run directly over him for no reason at all. Well, what the hell, all things had to end, both good and bad. There were other things in this world besides getting to step on somebody. The main thing was to hold on and not let it bother you. Joe Lon turned on his lights and drove off into the early November dusk.

He had been drinking most of the day, but he didn't feel drunk. He drove out past the empty flag pole on the post office and past the jail, where he saw Buddy Matlow's supercharged Plymouth with the big sheriff's star painted on the door parked under a leafless Chinaberry tree, and on through town, where several people waved to him. He didn't wave back. Finally, two people shook their gourds at him though and he did raise his hand and smile but he only half saw them. He was preoccupied by the thought of going home to Elfie and the babies, that trailer where he lived in a constant state of suffocating anger.

He had the trailer just outside of town on the edge of a ten-acre field he'd bought and turned into a combination trailer park and campground. He drove slowly down the narrow dirt road leading to it and passed finally under a big banner that he himself had strung from two tall telephone poles he had bought secondhand from the REA. The banner was neatly printed in letters about two feet high: WELCOME TO MYSTIC GEORGIA'S ANNUAL RATTLESNAKE ROUNDUP.

The lights were on in his trailer, a double-wide with a concrete patio, and he could see the shadow of his wife Elfie moving behind the window in the kitchen. He parked the truck, took the burlap sack from the back, and walked out to a little fenced-in pen that had a locked gate on it. He took out a key and opened it. In the back of the pen were several metal barrels. The tops of the barrels were covered with fine-mesh chicken wire. He kicked two of the barrels and immediately the little enclosure was filled with the dry constant rattle of diamondbacks. He took a stick with a wire hook on the end of it from the corner of the pen, set the burlap sack down, and waited.

The mouth of the sack moved and the blunt head of a rattlesnake appeared. It seemed to grin and waved its forked tongue, testing, tasting the air. There was an undulation and another foot of snake, perhaps four inches thick, appeared behind the head. Joe Lon moved quickly and surely and the snake was twisting slowly on the end of the hooked stick.

"Surprise, motherfucker," said Joe Lon, and dropped it into one of the barrels.

For a long moment, he stared into the barrel after the snake but all that appeared there was a writhing of the darkness, an incessant boiling of something thick and slow-moving.

He put the chicken wire back in place, threw the hooked stick in the corner of the pen, and headed for the trailer.

Elfie was at the sink when he walked into the kitchen. From the back she still looked like the girl he'd married. Her hair was red and glowed like a light where it fell to the small of her back. Her hips were round and full without being heavy. Her calves were high, her ankles thin. But then she turned around and she was a disaster. Those beautiful ball-crushing breasts she'd had two years ago now hung like enormous flaps down the front of her body. And although she was not fat, she looked like she was carrying a basketball under her dress. Two inches below her navel her belly just leaped out in this absolutely unbelievable way. The kitchen smelled like she had been cooking baby shit.

"Smells like you been cooking baby shit in here, Elf," he said.

There was a fat eighteen-month-old boy strapped into a highchair. Right beside him in a blue bassinet was a fat two-month-old boy.

Elfie turned from the sink and smiled. Her teeth had gone bad. The doctor said it had something to do with having two babies so close together.

"Joe Lon, honey, I been trying to keep your supper warm for you."

"Goddammit, Elf," he said. "You ever gone git them teeth fixed or not? I given you the money."

She stopped smiling, pulling her lips down in a self-conscious way. "Joe Lon, honey, I just ain't had the time, the babies and all."

There was no dentist in Mystic. She would have to go over to Tifton, and the trip took the better part of a day.

"Leave them goddam younguns with somebody and git on over there and git you mouth looked after. I'm sick and tard of them teeth like that."

"Aw right, Joe Lon, honey." She started putting food on the table and he sat down across from the two babies. "Don't you want to wash you hands or nothing?"

"I'm fine the way I am."

She took some thin white biscuits out of the oven and put them in front of him. Along with everything else she was a terrible cook. He took one of the lardy biscuits off the plate, tore it open, and dipped some redeye gravy on it. She sat with her plate in front of her without eating, just staring at him, her lips held down tight in an unseemly way.

"Was it a bad day at the store, Joe Lon, honey?"

He had been all right when he came into the trailer, but he sat at the table now trembling with anger. He had no idea where the anger came from. He just felt like slapping somebody. He wasn't looking at her but he knew she was still watching him, knew her plate was still empty, knew her mouth was trembling and trying to smile. It made him sick with shame and at the same time want to kill her.

"I left the nigger at the store," he said. "I went snake hunting."

The biscuit and gravy was sticking in his throat and a great gaseous bubble of whiskey rose to meet it. He wasn't going to be able to finish it. He wasn't going to be able to eat anything.

"What all did you git?" she said in a small voice. When he didn't answer, she said: "Did you git anything?"

The baby strapped in the highchair had a tablespoon he was beating the tray in front of him with. Then he quit beating the tray and threw it into the bassinet and hit the other baby in the head, causing him to scream in great gasping sobs. It so startled the baby in the highchair that he started kicking and screaming and choking too. Joe Lon, who had felt himself on the edge of exploding anyway, shot straight out of his chair. He grabbed the greasy biscuit off his plate and leaned across the table. Elfie didn't move. She left her hands in her lap. Her eyes didn't even follow him up. She kept staring straight ahead while he stuffed the dripping biscuit down the front of her cotton dress, between her sore, hanging breasts. He put his face right in her face.

"I got sompin," he shouted. "You want me to tell you what I got? I got goddammit filled up to here with you and these shitty younguns."

She had never once looked at him and the only sign she made that she might have heard was the trembling in her mouth got faster. He kicked over a chair on the way out of the trailer, and before he even got through the door he heard her crying join the babies'. By the time he got to his truck the whole trailer was wailing. He leaned against the fender trembling, feeling he might puke. He almost never had an impulse to cry, but lately he often wanted to scream.

Screaming was as near as he could get to crying usually, and now he had to gag to keep from howling like a moon-struck dog.

Jesus, he wished he wasn't such a sonofabitch. Elf was about as good a woman as a man ever laid dick to, that's the way he felt about it. Of course getting married with her three months gone and then putting another baby to her before the first one was hardly six months old didn't do her body any good. And it ruined his nerves completely. Hell, he guessed that was to be expected. But it didn't mean he ought to treat her like a dog. Christ, he treated her just like a goddam dog. He just couldn't seem to help it. He didn't know why she stayed with him.

He stood watching the ten-acre campground, knowing tomorrow it would fill up with snakehunters and blaring radios and noise of every possible kind and wondered if his nerves would hold together. He took a deep breath and held it a long time and then slowly let it out. There was no use thinking about it. It didn't matter one way or the other. The hunt was coming—the noise and the people—and whether he could stand it or not wouldn't change a thing. What he needed was a drink. He glanced once at the trailer, where the shadowy figure of his lumpy wife moved in the lighted window, and jumped into the truck and roared off down the road as though something might have been chasing him.

By the time he got to the store he had gone to howling. Through the open front door, he could see George sitting behind the counter on a high stool. There were no cars or trucks out front. Joe Lon sat next to the little store that was hardly more than a shed and howled. He knew George would hear him and it bothered him but George had heard him before. George would not say anything. That was the good thing about a nigger. He never let on that he saw anything or heard anything.

Finally Joe Lon got out of the truck and went inside. He didn't look directly at George because howling made him look just like he'd been crying, made his eyes red and his nose red and his face flushed. He was wishing now he had not torn up Berenice's letter. He wished he had it to look at while he drank a beer.

"Git me a beer, George," he said.

George got off the stool and went through a door behind the counter into a tiny room not much bigger than a clothes closet. Joe Lon sat on the high stool and hooked the heels of his cowboy boots over the bottom rung. He took out some Dentyne and lit a Camel. Directly, George came back with a Budweiser tallboy.

"What'd you sell today?" Joe Lon said.

"Ain't sell much," said George

"How much?" he said. "Where's you marks?"

George took a piece of ruled tablet paper out of the bib of his overalls. The paper had a row of little marks at the top and two rows of little marks at the bottom. It meant George had sold twenty bottles of beer, five half pints, fourteen pints, and one fifth, all bonded. He had also sold ten Mason fruit jars of moonshine.

"Hell, that ain't bad for a Thursday," said Joe Lon.

"Nosuh, it ain't bad for a Thursday," George said.

"I got it now," said Joe Lon. "You go on home."

George stood where he was. His gaze shifted away from Joe Lon's face until he was almost looking at the ceiling. "Reckon I could take me a little taste of sompin? Howsomever, it be true I ain't got no cash money."

Joe Lon said: "Take yourself one of them half pints a shine. I'll put it on you ticket. Bring me one of them bonded whiskeys while you in there."

George brought the whiskey and set it on the counter in front of Joe Lon, dropping as he did the half pint of moonshine into the deep back pocket of his overalls.

Joe Lon had brought another ruled piece of tablet paper out of a drawer in front of him. "Damned if you ain't drinking it up bout fast as you making it, George."

"I know I is," George said.

"You already behind on the week and it ain't nothing but Thursday," said Joe Lon.

"It ain't nothing but Thursday an I already be behind on the week," said George, shaking his head.

George hadn't moved so Joe Lon said: "You don't want to borrow money too, do you? You already behind."

"Nosuh, I don't want no money. I already behind."

"What is it then?"

"Mistuh Buddy. He done locked up Lottie Mae again."

"Jesus."

"Yessuh."

"For what?"

"Say she a sportin lady."

"Jesus."

"Yessuh."

Buddy Matlow would take a liking to a woman and if she would not come across he would lock her up for a while, if he could. As soon as he had been elected Sheriff and Public Safety Director for Lebeau County he started locking up ladies who would not come across. They were usually black but not always. Sometimes they were white. Especially if they were transients just passing through, and a little down on their luck. If he got to honing for one like that and she wouldn't come across, he'd lock her up no matter what color she was, sometimes even if she had a man with her. He had been called to accounts twice already by an investigator from the governor's office, but as he kept telling Joe Lon, they'd never touch him with anything but a little lecture full of bullshit about how he ought to do better. Hadn't he been the best defensive end Georgia Tech ever had? Hadn't he been consensus All-American two years back-to-back and wouldn't he have been a hell of a pro if he hadn't blown his right knee? And hadn't he gone straight to Veet Nam, stepped on a pungy stick that had been dipped in Veet Nam Ease shit? Hadn't they had to cut his All-American leg off? Goddammit he'd paid his dues, and now it was his turn.

"I'll see about it," Joe Lon said.

"Would you do that, Mistuh Joe Lon? Would you see about it?"

"I'll talk to him tonight or first thing in the morning."

"I wisht you could axe him about Lottie Mae tonight."

"Tonight or first thing in the morning."

He cut the seal on the whiskey with his thumbnail and took a pull at it. George started for the door. Joe Lon waved the bottle in the air and gasped a little. He'd taken a bigger swallow than he meant to. He followed the whiskey with a little beer while George waited, watching him patiently from the door.

"Lummy git them Johnny-on-the-spots?"

Lummy was George's brother. They both worked for Joe Lon Mackey. They'd worked for Joe Lon's daddy before they worked for Joe Lon. They'd never been told what they made in wages. And they had never thought to ask. They only knew at any given moment in the week whether they were ahead or behind on what they'd drawn on account. Ahead was good; behind was bad. Everybody was usually behind on everything though and nobody worried about it much.

When George didn't answer, Joe Lon said: "The Johnny-on-the-spots, did Lummy git'm?"

Nothing showed in George's face. He said: "Them Johnny-on-the-spot." It wasn't a question. He'd just repeated it.

"Hunters'll start coming in tomorrow," said Joe Lon. "If the Johnny-on-the-spots ain't in the campground we in trouble."

"Be in trouble," said George.

"What?" said Joe Lon.

George said: "What it was?"

"The shitters, George!" said Joe Lon. "Did Lummy git the goddam shitters or not?"

George's face opened briefly, relaxed in a smile. He did a little shuffle with his feet, took the moonshine out of his back pocket, looked at it, felt of it, and put it back. "Sho now, Lummy come wif the shitters on the truck all the way from Cordele."

"I didn't see'm on the campground," Joe Lon said. "I should've seen'm."

"He ain't taken them shitters offen the truck, but he have'm everone. I seen'm mysef. Mistuh Joe Lon, them shitters be fine."

"Just so you got'm, and they out there when the hunters start rolling in."

"You drink you whiskey, Mistuh Joe Lon. Don't think twice. Lummy and me is put our minds on the whole thing."

The screen door banged shut behind him, and Joe Lon poured another dollop of whiskey down. It wasn't doing any good much, didn't seem to be taking hold. He knew nothing was going to help a whole lot until he saw Berenice and either made a fool of himself or did not. He had the overwhelming feeling that he was going to make a fool of himself. Tear something up. Maybe his life. Well, at least he got the Johnny-on-the-spots. Last year it had taken two weeks to clean the human shit up in Mystic. There'd been about three times as many people as there had ever been before.

The rattlesnake roundup had been going on now as long as anybody in town could remember, but until about twelve years ago it had been a local thing, a few townspeople, a few farmers. They'd have a picnic, maybe a sack race or a horse-pulling contest and then everybody would go out into the woods and see how many diamondbacks they could pull out of the ground. They would eat the snakes and drink a little corn whiskey and that would do it for another year.

But at some time back there, the snake hunt had started causing outsiders to come in. Word got out and people started to come, at first just a few from Tifton or Cordele and sometimes as far away as Macon. From there on it had just grown. Last year they had two people from Canada and five from Texas.

Mystic, Georgia, turned out to be the best rattlesnake hunting ground in the world. There were prizes now for the heaviest snake, the longest snake, the most snakes, the first one caught, the last one caught. Plus there would be a beauty contest. Miss Mystic Rattler. And shit. Human shit in quantities that nobody could believe. This year, though, they had the Johnny-on-the-spots. Chemical shitters.

The telephone rang. It was his daddy. He wanted Joe Lon to send over a bottle with George.

"Ain't here," he shouted into the phone. "He already gone."

"Send somebody else then. Damn it all anyhow, I want a drink."

"Ain't nobody here but me. What happened to that bottle I left by this morning?"

"I drapped it and broke it."

"Bullshit."

"Joe Lon, I'm gone have to shoot you with a gun someday, talking to you daddy like that."

"Who'd run the store if you done that? Maybe Beeder could run the goddam store. Tote you goddam whiskey. Maybe she'd quit with the TeeVee and act normal. Send her over here right now and I'll give her a bottle for you."

"You a hard man, son, making such talk about you only sister. Lord Christ Jehovah God might see fit to strike you."

Joe Lon wanted to scream into the telephone that it was not Lord Christ Jehovah God that struck his sister. But he did not. It would do no good. They'd been over that too many times already.

"All right," he said finally, "never mind. I'll bring the whiskey myself. Later."

"How later?"

"When I git a chance."

"Hurry, son, my old legs is a hurtin."

"All right."

Just as he put the telephone down, a car drove up. It stopped but nobody got out. Carload of niggers. He sighed. Joe Lon Mackey carrying shine for a carload of niggers. Who would have thought it? He looked down at his legs as he was going into the little room behind the counter. Who would have thought them wheels, wheels with four-five speed for forty yards, would have come to this in the world. Well, anything was apt to come to anything in this goddam world. That's the way the world was. He spat as he took down the half pints of shine from the shelf.

During the next hour he sold more than had been sold all day, most of it to blacks who drove up and stopped under the single little light hanging from a pole in front of the store. He wished to God they were allowed to come inside so he wouldn't have to cart it out front to them. Of course, they *were* allowed to come inside. Except they were not *allowed* to come inside. It had been that way for the twenty years his daddy had run the store and it had been that way ever since Joe Lon had taken it over. He hadn't really *kept* it that way. It had just *stayed* that way. Nobody ever complained about it because if you wanted to drink in Mystic, Georgia, you had to stay on the good side of Joe Lon Mackey. Lebeau County was dry except for beer, and since Joe Lon had an agreement with the bootlegger, his was the only place within forty miles you could buy you a drink.

He worked steadily at the whiskey in front of him, chasing it with beer, and by the time Hard Candy's white Corvette car pulled up out front, he was feeling a little better about the whole thing. The Corvette was Berenice's old car and it reminded Joe Lon of everything he had been trying not to think about. Willard came in ahead of Hard Candy. He was an inch taller than Joe Lon and looked heavier. He had a direct lidless stare and tiny ears. His hair was cut short and his round blunt head did not so much sit on his huge neck as it seemed buried in it. He was wearing Levis and a school T-shirt with a tiny snake printed over his heart. His worn-out tennis shoes didn't have any laces in them. He sat on a stool across the counter from Joe Lon and they both watched Hard Candy come through the door stepping in her particular, high-kneed walk that always seemed to make her prance. She took a stool next to Willard. Nobody had spoken. They all sat, unsmiling, looking at one another.

Finally Willard said: "Me'n Hard Candy's just bored as shit."

Joe Lon said: "I got a fair case of the cain't-help-its mysef."

"I don't guess a man could git a goddam beer here," said Willard.

"I guess," said Joe Lon.

"Two," said Hard Candy.

Joe Lon said: "Hard Candy, if you don't quit walking like that somebody's gone foller you out in the woods and do sompin nasty to you."

"I wish to God somebody would," she said.

"*Somebody* already has," said Willard.

Joe Lon got up to get the beer. When he came back he said: "You want to hold this whiskey bottle I got?"

"We et us some drugs to steady us," Willard said. "I don't guess I ought to drink nothing harder'n beer."

"Okay."

"But I will," Willard said.

"I thought you might," Joe Lon said.

"You shouldn't do that," Hard Candy said.

Willard bubbled it four times and set it on the counter. Hard Candy took it up.

"We'll probably die," she said, a little breathless when she put it down.

"Probably."

They sat watching the door for a while, listening to the screenwire tick as bugs flew against it.

"I think it's gone be a shitty roundup," said Joe Lon.

"Will if this hot weather holds," Willard said. "Must be fifty degrees out there right now. Shit, it's like summer. Won't be a snake nowhere in the hole stays this warm."

They sat and watched the door again. A car passed on the road beyond the light now and then. Hard Candy turned and looked at Joe Lon.

"You reckon we could feed one?" she said.

"Let's wait a little while," Joe Lon said. "Maybe somebody'll come in we can take some money off."

"You got one back there that'll eat you think?" asked Willard.

"I try to keep one," Joe Lon said.

They watched the door some more.

"Hell, it ain't nobody coming," said Willard. "Git that rascal out here and let'm do his trick."

"I'll bet with you," said Hard Candy. She opened the little clutch purse she was carrying and bills folded out of the top of it.

"I don't take money from my friends," said Joe Lon.

"If you gone bet with him on the snake," said Willard, "you might as well go ahead and give him the goddam money anyway. You sure as hell ain't gone beat him."

"I lose sometimes," said Joe Lon, smiling.

"Git the goddam snake," said Willard. "Shit, I'll bet with you."

"You ain't bettin with me," said Joe Lon.

"I'll make you bet with me," said Willard.

They were both off their stools now, kind of leaning toward each other across the counter. They were both smiling, but there was an obvious tension in the attitude of their bodies.

"You ever come to make me do something," said Joe Lon, "you bring you lunch. You'll be staying awhile."

"Maybe I can think of something you'll *want* to bet on," said Willard.

"Maybe," said Joe Lon.

He went into the small room at the back of the counter and they followed him. There was a dim light burning. It took a moment for their eyes to adjust. Bottles of various sizes lined the shelves of both sides of the room. One middle shelf toward the back had no bottles on it. It held, instead, five wire cages that were about two feet square and about that high. Four of the cages held a rattlesnake. The fifth cage had several white rats in it. Joe Lon slapped the side of one of the cages with his hand. The snake made no move or sound. Nor did any of the other snakes.

"I've had these so long I probably could handle'm," said Joe Lon.

"Why don't you," said Willard Miller, showing his even, perfect teeth.

"Would if I wanted to," said Joe Lon.

"Hell, let's make that the bet then," said Willard. "The loser has to kiss the snake."

Joe Lon looked at him for a long moment. "You couldn't beat me at that either."

Willard Miller said: "I can beat you at anything." He was still smiling but something about the way he said it had no smile in it at all.

"You better back you ass out of here before you git it overloaded," said Joe Lon.

"If we don't never bet on nothing, how you know I cain't beat you?" said Willard.

"I know," said Joe Lon.

Hard Candy said: "I'll git the rat."

She went to the cage, opened the top, and reached in. When her hand came out she had a white rat by its long smooth pink tail. It hung head down without moving, its little legs splayed and rigid in the air. They followed Joe Lon out of the room to the counter, where he set the caged snake down.

"Ain't he a beautiful sumbitch?" said Joe Lon.

"Ain't nothing as pretty as a goddam snake," Willard said.

"I'm pretty as a snake," said Hard Candy.

They both looked at her. She was playing with the rat on the counter, holding its tail and letting it scratch for all it was worth. With her free hand she thumped the rat good-naturedly on top of its head.

"You almost are," said Willard, taking a pull at Joe Lon's whiskey bottle, "but you ain't quite."

Joe Lon took the bottle. "He's right, you ain't quite pretty as a snake."

"What would you two shitheads know about it anyway?" she said.

Joe Lon took a stopwatch from under the counter. It was the watch his coach had given him when he broke the state record for the two-twenty.

"Just for the fun what would you say?" asked Joe Lon.

"He'll hit the rat in a hundred and four seconds. He'll have it swallered in three and a half minutes."

"That's three and a half minutes *after* he hits it?"

"Right," said Willard.

Joe Lon bent down until his nose was only a half inch from the wire cage. The snake was in a corner, tightly knotted, with only its head and tail free. Its waving tongue constantly stroked in and out of its mouth. Its lidless eyes looked directly back at Joe Lon. The head was wide, wider than the body, and flat with a kind of sheen to it that suggested dampness. The tail was rigid now but still not rattling.

"This sucker'll hit right away, maybe twenty seconds. Yeah, I say twenty seconds. That rat'll be gone, tail and all, in two and a half minutes. That's total time. So I'm saying two minutes ten seconds after the hit." He had been staring into the cage while he talked. Now he straightened and backed off. "Drop that little fucker in."

"I'm playing," said Hard Candy.

"You already got the rat messed up and confused from thumpin him on the head," said Willard. "Stop thumpin him and do like Joe Lon says."

She held the rat up in the palm of her hand. She stroked its head with her thumb, gently. She pursed her lips and whispered to the rat: "Nobody's gone hurt you, little rat. We just gone let the snake kill you a little."

There was a spring-hinged door at the top of the cage that opened only one way. She set the rat on top of the door. It opened inward and the rat dropped through. The door immediately swung shut again. Joe Lon started the stopwatch. The rat landed on its feet, turned, and sniffed its pink tail. It looked at the snake in the corner, sat up on its hind legs, and started licking its front paws. The thick body of the snake moved and a high striking curve appeared below its wide blunt head.

None of them saw the strike; rather, they saw the body of the rat lurch as though struck by some invisible force. It sat for a split second without moving and then leaped straight into the air and landed on its back. The rattlesnake had retreated to the corner, its body again knotted and seemingly coiled about itself with only the dry flat head clear.

Almost immediately the snake came twisting out of the spot where it had withdrawn and very slowly approached the still rat. It touched the rat's back, ran its blunt head along the hairy stomach and legs, seemed to be taking the rat's measure. Finally, the snake opened its mouth, unhinged its lower jaw and, slow and gentle as a lover, seemed to suck the rat's head in over the trembling, darting tongue. Just as the head disappeared, the door of the store slammed open and a voice bellowed: "I caught you fuckers being cruel to little animals agin!"

They all turned together to see Buddy Matlow, wearing a cowboy hat and a wooden leg, standing in the doorway. When they looked back at the cage, there was nothing showing of the rat but the tail, long, pink, and hairless, sticking out of the snake's mouth like an impossible tongue.

"You degenerate sumbitches," Buddy Matlow said, watching the thin hairless tail disappear into the snake. "Never could understand how anybody could stand doing things like that to little animals."

"Ain't done nothing yet," said Joe Lon. "Snake et supper. We just watched."

"I ain't gone report you," said Buddy Matlow. "I just fed that snake of mine over at the jail not more'n an hour ago. You can git me a tallboy and a glass a that shine."

Joe Lon said: "How many times I got to tell you I don't sell nothing by the glass."

"I didn't think to pay for it," said Buddy.

"Makes a lot of noise for a goddam cripple, don't he," said Willard Miller. "I didn't have no more sense than to step on a stick with slopehead shit all over it, damned if I wouldn't say please when I asked for something." Willard's thin mouth was smiling almost shyly over the rim of his beer can, but his dark eyes were flat and hard and without light.

"You been running over too many grunions and reading about it in the *Wire Grass Farmer*," Buddy said. He looked down and casually examined his stump. "One of these days I'm gone have to stick this piece a oak up you ass and examine you liver."

Sitting between them, Hard Candy took another pull at the whiskey bottle. She was flushed from the speed they'd eaten and a little lacquer of sweat beaded her upper lip. She was enjoying it all a lot and only wished it was real, wished they would suddenly lunge off the stools and lock up on the bare wooden floor one on one, wished she could smell a little blood. But she knew it wouldn't come to anything. They might as well have been talking about the weather.

"You want sompin back here, Willard?" Joe Lon stood in the door of the little room with a beer in one hand and a water glass full of moonshine in the other.

Willard drained the beer in front of him and set it down. "Me'n and Hard Candy got to go." He smiled and blew Joe Lon a kiss as he and Hard Candy slid off their stools.

Joe Lon and Buddy Matlow watched Hard Candy leave.

She might as well have been in front of the band with her baton. She was all high knees and elbows, her hard little body jerking rhythmically. When they were gone, Joe Lon brought the beer and the glass to Buddy.

"You don't reckon you could put this goddam snake up do you?" Buddy said. "I just soon do my drinking without it."

They both looked down at the cage at the place where the rat had stopped in a thick knot about four inches deep in the snake. Joe Lon stood listening to the Corvette go over the gravel and onto the highway in a great roar and squalling of tires, laying two hundred yards of rubber before it took second gear. Only then did Joe Lon take up the cage and put it in the back room. He brought another beer back for himself and sat on a stool across the counter from Buddy Matlow.

"That boy's sompin, ain't he?" Buddy said.

"Uh huh."

They drank in silence for a while, listening to the night tick against the screens.

"I wish you'd drink and git the hell out of here. Ain't no niggers gone come up here with you car parked out there."

But what he said was reflex. It was what he always said. He wasn't studying the car with the sheriff's star on the door or Buddy Matlow. He was thinking about that Corvette, the squalling rubber, squatting with power when you floored it. It had belonged to Berenice before she went off to college. He used to drive it, used to make it sing on all the highways of Lebeau County. He knew where Willard was headed right this moment. He used to go there himself. It was all part of the package, part of being the Boss Snake of all the Mystic Rattlers. Willard was headed for Doctor Sweet's drug cabinet to which Hard Candy would have a key, just as Berenice had had one. They would get in there and Willard would eat whatever he felt like—a little something to take him up, or maybe bring him down a bit—and she would fill her little pockets full and off they would go over the dark countryside trying to decide what to do with the night.

That was the only decision there was once upon a time: what to do with the night. But then Berenice had graduated and the doctor had bought her an Austin-Healy and given Hard Candy the Vette and Berenice had gone off to the University of Georgia and Joe Lon had taken over from his daddy dealing whiskey. He tried to turn loose the memory but couldn't. He looked at Buddy, his cowboy hat pushed back on his head, quietly sipping out of the water glass, his eyes half closed and seeing nothing while Joe Lon saw for no particular reason—except perhaps because of the letter he had left in shreds under the stands—a night before a snake hunt in his senior year when he already knew he was never going to college and that Berenice was, saw himself sad, his heart hurt, leaning against the door of the white Corvette and Berenice inside smiling up at him. They were both wired tight on Dexedrine and the look in her face was a little off-center, a little crazy, as it often was. Many times it was like that when she was straight and had eaten nothing.

"Let's go look at the snake pit," she had said.

"I don't care," he said. He kept thinking he'd never tote the pigskin again, that he was destined to deal nigger whiskey. He dropped into the car and took it up in a single mounting roar to a hundred and twenty, had in fact wrung the needle off the speedometer. But it brought no pleasure. He saw his life too clearly, knew too well where it was going, and all the time Berenice sat on the other side, her crazy face oblivious to the speed, flashing her thighs and humming Dixie a little high and off-key. He had always loved her because she was crazy, didn't seem to give a damn about anything. Tonight he hated her for precisely those reasons.

The pit where all the snakes of the hunt would be kept was on the football field of Mystic High School, where it had always been since the hunt began. The Vette came onto the field in a growling power slide. The high rooster tail of sand thrown by the car was bright, glittering under a full moon. The shadows of the two enormous oak trees lay on the edge of the field like two dark lakes. It was in the shadow of one of the trees that they finally stopped, but not before Joe Lon had roared in three tight circles within yards of the trunk of the tree.

He had been driving about two thirds unwrapped from the dope so he thumbed the top off a fresh bottle of Budweiser taken from a bucket of ice between Berenice's feet. He was laughing but there was no humor in it. It didn't even sound good-natured. "I like to run over that goddam tree."

"You should have," she said. "Get us a ramp and jump the thing like Evel what's-his-fucking-face."

He reached across and got another bottle of beer and opened it. "Here, press this to you face. It'll help you feelings."

She took the beer. "Nothing's gone help my feelings tonight," she said.

"I'll think of something," he said.

"I hope so."

"Never doubt the Boss Snake," he said. "I told you never to."

She said, "I forgot."

"Don't forget," he said.

He opened the door and got out of the car. She got out too and came around to stand beside him. Without speaking, but as if on signal, they walked to the center of the field and stood together looking off toward the school. It was made of red brick with four white columns in front. Across the front, cut into a slab of cement, was the legend: LEBEAU COUNTY CONSOLIDATED HIGH SCHOOL OF MYSTIC, GEORGIA. It was as bright as day in the moonlight and they stood in the field of packed dirt equidistant between the wood-and-wire snake pit on their left and another structure built of fresh-cut raw lumber on their right. The structure on the right was a kind of stage with a painted sign stuck on each of its four sides. All the signs said the same thing: THE RATTLESNAKE QUEEN.

"Take my dick out," said Joe Lon. "I have to piss."

Without even looking, but with no fumbling, she reached over with her left hand and unzipped his Levis. She held him while he gave water, a great frothing stream into the moon-colored dirt at their feet.

"Don't seem like to me this goddam year will ever be over," he said.

She shook him good while he talked and put him back behind the zipper.

He said: "Seem like I been in this town forever."

"It'll be different," she said, "at the university. Anyway, I hope it'll be different for me. I could stand me something different for a while."

She was going to the University at Athens in the fall to be the meanest majorette the state of Georgia had ever seen. And they pretended he was going to the University of Alabama to break bones for Bear Bryant, although they both knew he wasn't going anywhere but to the little store where his daddy kept the back room full of bootleg whiskey.

"That's nine months away," he said. "Anything that long might as well be never."

"I'll miss you," she said.

"Uh huh. I magine."

"Anybody that's known a Boss Snake'll never forget him."

As they talked they had wandered over to the snake pit.

Sheets of plywood formed the sides of a square about twenty feet long and twenty feet wide. The plywood rose to four feet and then chicken wire had been stretched on top of that. Two feet of earth had been dug out of the bottom of the pit. This was where the snakes would be weighed, marked, and collected during the hunt.

"I think I love you," she said. "I think I'll always love you."

He looked straight up toward the bright moon and started turning in slow circles. Finally he stopped and turned his unblinking, slightly drunken gaze on her. "You gone have to do sompin about this conversation. It's just boring the shit out of me."

"We could go to the car and get another beer," she said in a small sullen voice.

"We already done that," he said. "I don't feel like doing what we already done before."

He reached out and picked her up and put her under his massive arm. Her full cheerleader's legs dangled behind and she arched her back to look up at him. Her face was slack and without expression. He knew she was only mildly interested in what he might do. He was given to picking her up at odd moments and doing something with her.

He walked around on the other side of the plywood and wire pen. There was a little gate there with two metal hinges and a hook latch. He opened the gate. He held her under his left arm and with his right pointed down into the dirt pit.

"Look at them snakes," he said.

They stared down into hard-packed moon-colored dirt.

"It's enough poison in there to kill everthing in Mystic," she said.

"To kill everthing in the world," he said.

"Good," she said. "Rattlesnake fangs hanging from all the throats of the world."

"From titties," he said. "Them fanged mouths sucking them titties."

"Chewing dicks," she said.

"Being dicks," he said and stepped down into the pit. "Snakes and dicks. Sweet slick dicks and snakes."

"Put me down in the snakes," she said.

He laid her down on the dirt floor of the pit on her back. She writhed gently looking up at him. His moon-struck hair splayed from his head.

"Oh God, your snakes are cold." She touched her belly. "They're here. They're filling me here." She touched her breasts. "And here." Her eyes were closed now. Her mouth a little way open. "A cold bath of snakes," she said. "I'm freezing full of snakes. All in my blood. Crawling through my heart." She opened her eyes and he still stood above her, beautiful and powerful with the moonlight splintering against his back, casting his face in solid shadow. "Lie down here, Joe Lon. Lie down in these snakes."

He drew back. "No." She was a crazy bitch, had always been, and she sometimes scared him. She was always doing crazy shit and saying crazy shit, and sometimes it scared him. Sometimes out in the black dark when she started in on it, he felt something go soft and queasy in his stomach.

"You scared," she said. "You scared of these snakes?"

Joe Lon said: "I ain't scared of a goddam thing. Don't matter if it walks or crawls or flies in the air."

"Then lie down. I'm cold. I'll die in these freezing snakes."

He should have kicked her or stepped on her but he didn't. He slowly sank to his knees and then lowered himself over her. They lay very still for a while. Then he moved and lay beside her on his back.

"Feel'm?" she said. "Feel them snakes?"

He made a sound, a kind of neutral grunt.

"We're buried to our goddam eyes in the thick good

bodies of snakes," she said. "And you'll die too. You might as well go on, Joe Lon, go on and be afraid."

She was touching him now, with both hands, tentatively, squeezing and pressing, her fingers extended with the tips together, moving over his body like the twin heads of blind snakes, or so it seemed to him, lying there in a cold sweat.

Her hands stopped and she crawled up over him, deliberately making her body twist and writhe in the supple windings of a snake. She started again touching him. She was moving all over now, her legs, her body, her hands. Then everything quieted, everything seeming to stop at once.

"I found him," she whispered. "The Boss Snake of all the snakes."

Joe Lon lay on his back, his eyes tightly closed, the skin on his wide face drawn and white. "You goddam right," he whispered.

"Look," she said. "Oh look at him. That sumbitch strike you, you know you struck."

He opened his eyes and raised his head and looked down himself to the place where she had unzipped his Levis and his cock stood curved in front of her face. She hissed and he felt her hot breath. Her tongue, black in the shadow of her hair, darted in and out of her mouth.

He put his head back and said: "Okay."

He closed his eyes and thought about the hand job she had given him under the east stands of the practice field when she was in the tenth grade and then the first time he had asked her for a date and they were in his Ford pickup, parked and kissing to the point of exploding there behind the R&W Rootbeer stand in Tifton where they had driven on a Friday night to first see a movie because there was no movie in Mystic and then go for a hamburger they never got because he reached over and dragged her in with him behind the steering wheel and they had started kissing and trembling and going at each other with both hands and it had been the same ever since. All the way through high school they had been at each other as though they were fighting a war.

Lying there in the snakepit, they both heard the sound of a car motor a long time before they knew it was actually coming onto the football field with them, and they were being hit by the gravel and sand raining through the chicken wire before they knew the car was spinning around and around the place where they lay.

Joe Lon straightened up and Berenice came up behind him and they saw Buddy Matlow's patrol car at the same time. Buddy hung out the window grinning, and whooping at the top of his lungs.

"Goddammit," he screamed at them as he one-handed the Plymouth around and around the pit where they sat hunkered, turning to follow him, "goddammit, ain't life grand!"

In the car beside him, a woman, small and dark, sat very still and did not turn her head.

"Crazy bastard's got another one," Joe Lon said. But Berenice had already lowered herself upon him again and did not answer.

"How's at?"

"What?" said Joe Lon. When he looked up from his beer, Buddy Matlow was watching him from across the counter.

"You better go on home, son," said Buddy Matlow, "you started talking to you beer."

"Just thinking out loud," Joe Lon said.

"Who was the crazy fucker answering you?" said Buddy.

Joe Lon shrugged and looked at the ceiling. The night was beginning to get cool. Joe Lon got up and went over to the window and closed it. "You want another beer?"

"I could drink another one, if it was give to me."

Joe Lon brought it out of the back room. Buddy still had half a glass of moonshine. He took a sip and chased it.

Joe Lon said: "You wouldn't want to let Lottie Mae go home, would you?"

"What?"

"Buddy, I'm too tired and hurt to talk about it."

"Don't talk about it then," Buddy said. "I don't know as it's any of you business."

"It bothers the niggers. If it bothers them, it bothers me."

"How's at?"

"They unload the shitters. They hep me. I told George I'd speak to you."

"You real worried about George, are you?"

"He ain't the only one in the family. I don't even know how many connections they got and they all hep me out one way or the other. I said I'd speak to you."

"All right, you spoke to me."

"You wouldn't want to let her go home, would you?"

Buddy Matlow watched him steadily for a long moment, then he drained the water glass. "Sure," he said. "Okay. I'll send her home tonight."

"I prechate it," said Joe Lon.

Buddy Matlow reached for his back pocket where he had his wallet chained to his cartridge belt.

"On me," Joe Lon said. "I owe you."

"Decent of you," Buddy said. He turned and went out to his Plymouth Cruiser, where he sat behind the wheel smoking. His face was mottled and every now and then he spat out the window. He couldn't seem to cut any slack anywhere. He'd earned it. Goddammit, he *knew* he'd earned it but nobody would own up to it. If you couldn't cut a little slack behind a ruined All-American wheel—ruined in defense of the fucking U S of A, where *could* you cut it? He thumped the cigarette in a high sparking arch and pulled away from the store and drove slowly in a controlled rage to the jail. His deputy, Luther Peacock, was sitting at the desk when he got there.

"Go eat supper, Luther."

"How long you want me to eat?" Luther said.

"Eat till after midnight, Luther. You take you a good slow supper."

"I'm hongry anyhow," Luther said, reaching for his hat.

Buddy Matlow walked across the room and down a hall to a cell. He stopped without looking in it. "You know if you tell anybody I love you, I'll kill you. You know that, don't you?"

Lottie Mae did not answer. She sat on a low chair in the center of the cell as still and quiet as a rock. There was only one cell in the large bare room and she was the only prisoner. There were two windows but they were both closed. Sweat stood on Lottie Mae's face like drops of oil. Buddy Matlow walked up and down in front of the cell. There was no other sound but the steady knock of his peg leg against the floor.

"I ain't tellin nobody nothin," she finally said.

"You told George," he said. "You told George and he told Joe Lon and now I guess ever sumbitch in Mystic is laughing at old Buddy Matlow. An I'm gone tell you one goddam thing, Buddy Matlow don't like to be laughed at. He don't take to it one damn bit."

"I ain't tol George," she said.

"Well, what is it? Can he read goddam minds or what?"

"Ain't nobody in Mystic don't know where I is," she said.

Buddy Matlow quit walking. He took hold of the bars and stared at her. Her thin cotton dress stuck to her back and sweat ran on her bare legs.

"It won't make a difference whether they know or not," he said.

She got off the stool and came to stand in front of him. "Please, Mister Buddy, let me go on . . ."

"Goddam you, quit calling me Mister! Ain't I already told you I loved you?"

She went back to sit on the stool, walking backwards, never taking her eyes off him, her body shaking as if with cold.

When she had stopped shaking she said in a low sullen voice: "I ain't studying love. It's gone be trouble account all this. You be in trouble already now."

Buddy Matlow gripped the bars and stared at her. "*Be* in trouble? Why, bless your sweet nigger heart, I was born in trouble. It's been trouble ever since." He slapped his right thigh. "That's trouble right there. That fucking stick leg is trouble." He had been shouting, but his voice suddenly lowered. "But what the hell, I try not to whine about it too much. Everybody's got their load of shit to haul. Look at you. Ever time you show that black face in the world you got trouble. You think I don't know that? I do. I appreciate what it is to be a nigger. I got ever sympathy in the world for it. But the minute I laid eyes on that little jacked-up ass of yours I known I was in love again."

"Talking crazy," she said.

"I may *be* crazy," he said.

"Might as well let me out. I ain't doing nothing nasty. Didn't las time. Ain't this time."

"This time is different," Buddy Matlow said.

"Ain't never gone be different," she said. "My ma ain't raised no youngan of hern to do nothin nasty."

Buddy Matlow smiled. "Last time you was locked up we weren't having us a roundup."

"Roundup," she said.

"Snakes," he said.

"Snakes?" she said.

"Rattlesnakes."

"Lordy."

Buddy Matlow went over to one corner and bent down behind a splintered wooden desk. When he straightened up he had a metal bucket in his hand. A piece of screen wire was bent to cover the top of the bucket. He brought the bucket to the cell door and set it down.

"You know what's in that bucket?"

"Lordy Lordy Lordy Lordy Lordy." She sang the word in a little breathless whisper.

He turned the bucket over with his wooden leg and a diamondback as thick as a man's wrist and nearly four feet long spilled out onto the floor. It neither rattled nor lifted its head. Only its bright lidless eyes showed that it was alive. There was a knot in the snake's body, a swelling about a foot back from the head, like a tumor growing there.

"You ain't got a thing to be scared of, Lottie Mae, darling. This snake just et. Had'm a rat."

He touched the swelling in the snake's body with his wooden leg. The snake lifted its head, the tongue darting and quivering on the air. But there was no striking curve in its body and presently the head dropped back to the floor.

"The snake or me one is coming in there with you. Which you reckon?"

Lottie Mae did not answer. Her gaze had locked on the snake and had not once lifted from it. With his peg leg Buddy turned the snake's head between the bars. Slowly he pressed the thick body into the cell.

The first time she spoke Buddy couldn't make out what she said and had to tell her to say it again and when she said it loud enough for him to hear he made her say it again.

"I ruther you," she said, still looking at the snake. Her hand lifted to the top button of her cotton dress. "I ruther you."

Buddy said: "Ain't it a God's wonder what a snake can do for love?"

He had to go up to the desk for the key. When he got back she had her dress off and was lying on the narrow cot looking at the snake, which had not moved. Buddy took off his gun and his cartridge belt, took the steel-sprung black-jack out of his back pocket, all the time watching her while she watched the snake. He got naked but did not take off his peg leg.

"You a purty thing," he said softly and then fell on her with the kind of grunt he might have made if somebody had hit him.

He was quick and—for the rest of it—silent, his great weight lunging against her. The only parts of her that showed from under him were her hands, her raised knees, and her face turned off under the edge of his heaving chest, staring with glazed eyes at the snake, which looked back at her and did not blink.

"All right," he said, finally, "you can go now."

He banged his wooden leg steadily against the wall by the bed while he watched her slip the thin cotton dress over her head.

He called after her as she was going down the hall: "And don't let it happen again."

She walked out into the night and down the road toward the house where she lived with her mother. But she would remember none of it, not Buddy Matlow's smothering weight, or her bare feet on the stony road, or anything else. The snake had supplanted it all. Her head was filled with its diamond pattern and lidless eyes, and a terror was growing in her that was beyond screaming or even crying.

She went blindly down the single paved street of Mystic. The only light that was on was at BIG JOE'S CONFECTIONS.

It went off as if on signal as she was passing. Joe Lon saw her as he turned from locking the door. She was no more than twenty feet from him.

"Well," he said to himself, "ever now and then something goes right in this fucking world." He walked over to her and she stopped. "You all right, Lottie Mae?"

She said nothing and her face showed nothing and she did not look at him but straight ahead. There was nothing strange in that. They were very nearly the same age, and he had known her, more or less, all of his life. She had always been a shy, quiet girl. When she came with her mother to the house to work for his daddy, he could never remember her saying anything.

"I'm just going myself," he said. "You want a ride?" The place where she lived was almost a mile away. It was late but he was in no hurry to get home to Elfie. She glanced briefly at him and walked away. "No skin off my ass," he said.

He got into the truck with a bottle of whiskey. He knew the old man would be waiting for it, but he took his time anyway. The house where his daddy lived was old and tilted slightly to the left, with a wide porch running around three sides. It was two stories, with a second floor where nobody ever went, where his daddy stored furniture and old clothes and newspapers—the Atlanta *Constitution* and the Albany *Herald* and the Macon *Telegraph*—all of which the old man subscribed to and which came in the mail a day late and took up his mornings until he began drinking whiskey at noon. Joe Lon could have moved into the big house with his father and his sister, the old man even asked him to, offering to clean out the second floor and let him and Elfie have it, but Joe Lon would be damned and in hell before he would do that, and even though he loved his father, admired him, and could tolerate his sister, he knew that it would never work to try to live in the same house with them.

Among other reasons it wouldn't work was he liked to beat Elfie occasionally, or didn't like it, rather he couldn't help it, and his father would have killed him if he had ever found out he punched Elfie. More than once they had had to tell the old man that Elfie had fallen out of the door of the trailer onto her head when she turned up with two black eyes, or had run into the closet door or closed her hand in the stove oven, which actually once was true but it was because Joe Lon was holding her fingers there with one hand while he slammed the oven with the other. The old man told people everywhere that his daughter-in-law, Elf, was a goddam fine woman, good mother, but she was probably the clumsiest human being God ever made.

The old man was not a good man by anybody's reckoning; he just didn't hold with hurting women. He had once castrated a Macon pulpwood Negro who drove bootleg whiskey for him because the Negro had stolen a case off the truck. Another time he and one of his friends had scalped a white man for some reason that nobody ever knew and the old man had not disclosed. He also had probably the best pit bulldogs in all of Georgia, which were the pride of his life and which he loved deeply and which were the best fighting dogs because he treated them with a savage and unrelenting cruelty that even other pit bull owners could not bear to witness or emulate.

Joe Lon drove his pickup down the narrow lane bordered on both sides with the skeletoned limbs of winter-naked pecan trees. The huge house was dark except for the front room where the old man lived and the thin wavering light of his sister's television in a side room toward the back. Joe Lon didn't know what time it was but he knew it might be after midnight. He was drunk, but not good and drunk the way he liked to be. The whiskey simply had refused to take hold beyond a certain point. On the seat beside him were two quarts of bonded bourbon. There were no labels on the bottles. There never were. It tasted like Early Times. He thought it probably was, and it was also probably hijacked stuff. He'd gotten it for two dollars a bottle, a whole goddam trailer of it. He hadn't asked where it came from. He never did.

Joe Lon let himself in and went down the short hall to the room where his daddy sat with his back to the door watching a dog strapped onto an electric inclined treadmill. It was a standard training device for fighting dogs. His daddy was nearly deaf and he did not look up even though Joe Lon slammed the door. His daddy was named Joe Lon too but was called Big Joe, partly to distinguish the father from the son and partly because the old man was nearly seven feet tall. There wasn't a hair on his head but he had eyebrows that were thick and black and very long.

When Joe Lon came up behind the chair and leaned down and said into Big Joe's ear: "Here's the goddam whiskey," the bald head did not move at all but the eyebrows twitched, seemed actually to turn on his face.

"Bout time," said Big Joe. "I been sober since sundown."

"I magine," said Joe Lon. He had to shout to make himself heard.

He went over and sat in a ragged overstuffed chair. Big Joe broke the seal, raised the bottle, and took a tentative swallow. He brought the bottle down, looked at it, shook it gently, then handed it to his son.

"Git us that pitcher," said Big Joe, but Joe Lon had already gone to the sideboard, where there was a white crock pitcher beside a wash basin. He brought two short glasses and the pitcher of water. He poured a glass and gave it to his daddy. He had brought a glass for himself but he never did get around to pouring any water in it. He set the glasses on the floor beside the chair and did not look at it again.

"You ought to have a little water with that whiskey," said Big Joe.

"I been trying to git drunk," said Joe Lon, his voice flat and disinterested. "It don't seem to be working though."

They watched the dog on the treadmill. The sound of his breathing, wet and ragged and irregular, filled the room. There was no alternative for the dog but to run even though he had obviously gone as far as he could go, further even, because now and then his front legs collapsed and the treadmill kept turning and the dog's knees were scraped and ground against the electrical tread until somehow he regained his feet. The front of his legs was raw and bleeding. But the dog made no sound except for the irregular gasping gulps of air he managed to suck in over his lolling tongue. Part of the reason he made no sound was a weighted device strapped onto his lower jaw. It was to strengthen the snapping and chewing muscles and it had been hooked onto the animal's jaw most of the afternoon so that now the dog could no longer support the weight and his mouth was splayed as though ripped, as though it were a raw and bleeding wound.

"How's Elf?" said Big Joe.

"She ain't doing bad," said Joe Lon.

"She ain't run in to nothing else has she?"

"Not yet," Joe Lon said, "but shit you never can tell, she's apt to fuck herself up any time."

"She's a good woman, Elf is," said Big Joe, "and you a lucky man. You one lucky man and don't you ever forget that, Joe Lon."

"Shit no," said Joe Lon, "I ain't gone forget just how fucking lucky I am."

"You cuss too much for a boy," said Big Joe. He passed the bottle. "I never liked that word for cussing. Fucking is no kind of word for a man to use to cuss with."

Joe Lon didn't answer and they watched the dog, which had fallen, struggle back up from his battered knees again. Since he had been in the room the steady insistent sound of the television had been coming through the wall. Laughter, sudden and joyous, burst in and among the dog's breathing. His sister, Beatriz Dargan Mackey but called Beeder by anybody who had a chance to call her anything which was not often because she stayed pretty close to the Muntz, had on Johnny Carson. Johnny's sly badgering voice mixed nicely with the pit bull's bloody breathing because the dog had started hemorrhaging from the mouth now and it smoothed out the ragged edges of sound until it almost sounded like someone with a pleasant voice humming a sweet song a little off-key.

The old man whispered softly toward the dog now and flapped his batlike eyebrows: "Take it, you mean sumbitch. Do it! Work!" He crooned it in a little sing-song voice, the same words over and over again.

"How much longer you gone leave Tuff on the wheel?" asked Joe Lon.

"I don't know, and Tuff don't neither," said Big Joe. "But we'll both know when we git there." The old man shifted, seemed to squirm in the chair where he sat. "Listen, I'm sorry I was so hateful on the telephone when I called you about the whiskey tonight."

Joe Lon didn't answer. The whiskey was beginning to work. He was going to be able to get drunk and the knowledge lifted his heart. Suddenly, he wanted everybody to feel good, to get a break. Even the dog.

"Listen," said Joe Lon. "I think Tuff is taking a killing on that wheel."

The old man who had been crooning to the dog again stopped and said: "No, he ain't. He ain't taken a killing yet."

Tuff had survived four fights. He had long lightning-bolt scars, much darker than his brindle color, running back across his shoulders and back. One ear was split deeply and both ears had been chewed nubby. His broad forehead was a mass of grayish, welty scar tissue and his left eye, the one he was blind in, had no color demarcation in its solid milky surface. Tuffy was training for his fifth fight. They'd all been against the best stock in the South, and Big Joe had decided if he won to retire him to stud and a place of privilege in the kennel.

"Lummy and them git them bleacher seats fixed up at the pit?"

"I walked out there when I got up this morning," said Big Joe. "Weren't up then."

"I'll speak to George."

"Leave'm alone," said Big Joe. "I told him to do it. He said he'd do it. They'll be there when we need'm."

"I hope so."

"George and Lummy's puttin up them seats before you was born."

"You told me."

"Give me that whiskey bottle. You know why I git hateful, don't you?"

"Yeah, I know."

"If you had to listen to that goddam TeeVee going day in and day out, you'd be hateful too." Big Joe lifted the whiskey bottle to the light. It was a little more than half empty. "You didn't bring but one of these?"

"You drink too much. A man your age ought not drink like you do."

"A man my age ain't got a hell of a lot else to do."

"You got the dogs."

"Yeah, I got the dogs. And besides the dogs I got quiz shows and game shows and murder shows and funny shows and shit shows eighteen hours a day coming through ever wall in the house. I wish to God I could go the rest of the way deaf before she runs me the rest of the way crazy with the Muntz."

Joe Lon belched, and felt better than he'd felt in days. He stood up and tested his legs. "Well," he said, "it's cheaper'n a hospital."

"Yeah," said Big Joe, "it's that. But after you said that, it ain't nothing else to say." He was no longer passing the bottle. Now that it was half gone, he had put the cap back on it and put it under his chair. "I sometime think about seeing one more time if I cain't git the state to take her."

Joe Lon didn't like to even let himself think about his sister, but he didn't want her in a goddam state insane asylum either. "You'd feel funny going to a fight and everbody knowing Big Joe Mackey's given his only daughter up to the fucking state."

The old man waved his big hand and did not look at his son. "I ain't done it yet, have I? And God knows I been tried. I been tried severely and I ain't been found wanting."

"Well, don't feel too goddam good about it, it ain't over yet. You still got time to ruin everthing." His mood had shifted to something sour and mean, and he had felt it shift, like a load on a truck might shift, suddenly and with great force. He had always been given to such shifts in mood and temper but they had become more and more frequent and seemingly without cause the last year or so.

Big Joe said: "You started to church, you'd stop so much of that heavy cussing. And particular you'd stop using that word to cuss with. It ain't a fittin word for a man to use."

"I guess," said Joe Lon. His daddy was a deacon in The Church of Jesus Christ With Signs Following and was forever trying to get Joe Lon to start going. "I got to git on home. Maybe I'll see you tomorrow."

"If you don't, be sure and send the nigger over with something to drink."

"All right."

"You git them shitters?"

"I ain't seen'm," said Joe Lon, "but I been told they over by the grounds."

"Good, good. Make all that shit a lot easier to handle."

Joe Lon went through the door into the hall. He had had no intention of going in to see his sister, but once in the hall he turned to look in the direction of her room, where the thin light showed under the door. He felt a rush of pity at his heart for Beeder, who almost never saw anybody but the cook, who almost never left her damp room that smelled sweetly of mildewed sheets, and who would almost certainly end up in some bare white place behind a locked door with her own shit smeared over her face. He leaned back against the wall and closed his eyes and felt the hot start of tears and at the same time saw clearly his sister again as she had been in the tenth grade when he had been a stud junior running back, how pretty she had been behind the yellow pompons cheering for him and the team, doing complicated little maneuvers in the bright sun with the other girls, and even though he never actually decided to do it he was opening the door to her room where the familiar awful smell washed warmly over his face and he saw her propped in bed with the covers pulled up under her chin so that her shadowed face looked empty of eyes in the dim inconstant light from the television set.

He stopped at the foot of the bed. She cut her eyes up at him briefly and then looked back at the television, where Johnny and his guests were in convulsions.

"How you feeling, Beeder?" he said.

"He killed Tuffy yet?" she said, not looking at him.

"He ain't gone kill Tuffy."

"I wish to God he would. I know Tuffy wishes to God he would."

"But he won't."

"No," she said, "he won't kill us. If he'd just kill us all . . . But that's more than anybody can ask for, I guess." She pulled the blankets down from her chin. Her face was stark white and without expression in the light. "But you cain't ask for death. Anything else, maybe. But not death. You'd think it'd be just the other way round, wouldn't you? Joe Lon, *wouldn't you?*"

"I reckon," he said.

"How was the game?" she said.

"We won," he said.

"I know you won," she said. "I didn't ask for that. *How* did you win?"

"We ran at them, Beeder. We stuck it down their throat."

She turned her face away from him so that half her thin mouth was buried in the yellowing pillow. "That hurts. God, it hurts, that everthing is eating everthing else."

He sat on the edge of the bed and watched the Muntz. There was a Mexican comic on now, explaining how much fun it had been to grow up in a ghetto in Los Angeles. He made starving, and rats, and broken plaster, and getting beat on the head by cops just funny as shit. The audience was falling out of their seats. Johnny was wiping tears of laughter out of his eyes.

"They're out there now, you know, eating each other."

"I magine," he said without looking at her.

On the other side of the wall now a sound had started like the coughing of a very old, very sick man. They both knew that it was Tuffy and that it was not a cough at all but, rather, all that was left of his bark. He was exhausted and bleeding and having the life scraped out of him by the electric treadmill and it was the best bark he had left.

He turned from the television and looked at her. "Beeder," he said, "what . . . what is it that . . . what do you *think*?"

"Think," she said. "Think?"

"I mean, well, goddammit, Beeder, they ain't gone let you stay in here with the fucking Muntz for the rest of you life. Is that what you think, that they're gone let you stay in here," he pointed to the television, "watching that jack-off?"

"I'm not hurting nobody," she said. And then, her eyes going darker, her lips paler: "They gone make me leave, are they?"

"Christ almighty!" he said. He wished to hell he had the bottle of whiskey out of the truck. She watched him now instead of the television set, but her eyes were unsteady on him and kept sliding around the room as though she was looking for something she couldn't find. Ever since she'd started acting this way—ever since she'd gone nuts—Joe Lon had had the feeling that if he just jerked her up by the shirtfront and demanded that she act normal she would. He had in fact done it, more than once, usually when he was drunk or drinking, saying: "Goddammit, Beeder, you better act normal. Come on, quit playing around and be right." But it had not helped. He had never been able to shake the feeling though that if he caught her off guard and said just the right thing in just the right way, he would save her. He had the impulse to do it now. But instead he raised his eyes to the shelves behind her bed where all his trophies were. This had been his room once but she had taken it over when she went nuts. She had a room just like it across the hall and he had never known nor could she say why she had moved in here. He was already married to Elfie by then so it didn't really matter. Except it did. He seldom let himself think about it but he didn't like her in his goddam room, nuts or not, even though he no longer used or wanted the room. Even so, in every way that made any sense the room did not even belong to him anyway.

Maybe it was because of the trophies, the signed game balls that had been bronzed and mounted, the High School Back of the Year award for all of the state of Georgia, the certificate for playing in the High School All-American Game in Dallas, Texas, and two whole shelves of trophies and certificates from track. As a stranger might have, he watched them now above his sister's nearly covered face with only the dark hair and frightened eyes showing. They seemed, those bronzed images of muscled young men caught in straining, static motion, they seemed in no way to have anything to do with him, nor ever to have had anything to do with him.

They seemed in fact to have been an accident. Like his sister's madness. It had just happened. Nobody knew why or apparently would ever know. He was stronger and faster and meaner than other boys his age and for that he had been rewarded. He had even suspected that he was smarter, too. For whatever reason, though, the idea of *studying*, of sitting down and deliberately committing facts and relationships to memory was deeply repugnant to him. And always had been. Unless it had to do with violence. He liked violence. He liked blood and bruises, even when they were his own.

He always had his assignments when he went on the field. With no effort at all, he would memorize and run a dozen complicated pass patterns. And he not only knew his own assignment but he knew those of his teammates too. He learned not just the fundamentals of football but also the most delicate nuances, so that he was a vicious blocker, and ran probably the most awesome interference that his coach,

Tump Walker, had ever seen. It had all been terribly satisfy-
ing while it had been going on, but now it lived in his memory like a dream. It had no significance and sometimes in-
explicably he wished it had never happened.

He sighed and dropped his eyes to Beeder's face. She
was quietly and contentedly watching a picture of the American flag while a chorus of voices sang the National Anthem.
Then, as he looked at her, the flag went off and a man said
that concluded broadcast activities for the day and a screen
of snow and static came on and Beeder watched the snow
and listened to the static as though it had been just the most
interesting show in the world. He didn't know for sure, but
he thought she sometimes watched the snow and static all
night, right into the next morning when the Farm Report
came on at six o'clock and then watched that. If he could
believe his father she sometimes went on binges of television
that lasted for days without stopping. "Just like a goddam
drunk going on a spree," Big Joe would say.

"Beeder, when's the last time you been out of this room?"

She didn't answer, but she did momentarily look away
from the television.

"When's the last time you bathed youself?" Now she did
not look at him. "It stinks in here. You know it stinks in
here?"

She had a chamber pot under her bed that she sat on
instead of going to the bathroom down the hall and the
cook was supposed to empty it when she came in the morning and again before she left at night. Sometimes she did.
But sometimes she didn't. Joe Lon wondered if it was full
now, and although it was something he had never done
before, he bent and reached under the bed from where he
sat and pulled it out. He knew the pot was not empty before
he ever looked at it. It was full of water and on the surface
floated three dark turds.

He felt like howling. When he looked up she was watching him. Her mouth held a shy smile. "Beeder," he said in a pleading voice, "Beeder, you got to do something about . . ."

But he stopped because she was sitting up in her bed, pushing the covers back. She was wearing a dingy gown made of cotton. Her bones were insistent under the thin fabric and seemed as brittle as a bird's. She moved out from under the covers and across the bed until she was sitting beside him.

"I would kill it if I could," she said, and reached down and lifted a piece of shit and put it in her hair.

He had watched, unable to move, to believe either that she actually meant to do what he knew she meant to do. Putting shit in her hair was something he had never seen her do before. He had seen her do some pretty bad things but not that.

He got up and backed toward the door, refusing to let himself turn his face from her, saying as he went: "Lord help us all. Sister Beeder, Lord help us all." He had not called her Sister Beeder since they were children. She was already back in bed watching the snow, listening to the static before he got through the door.

In the truck, under the pecan trees bare and black in the bright heavy moon, he sat without turning on the motor or lights and let half a bottle of whiskey down his throat. He gagged against the whiskey but he held the bottle to his mouth anyway, feeling his stomach tighten against the warm bourbon. He could not shake the image of his sister easing her befouled head back into the pillow. But gradually it did recede. As he sat there in the dark hurting himself more and more—as much as he could stand—with the whiskey the memory of the whole evening grew unsure and lost all significance whatsoever.

Later—he wouldn't remember how much later—he saw

his daddy come through the door out onto the porch and come down the steps into the yard. He led Tuffy on a leash, the jagged lightning-bolt scars blacker in the bright moonlight. Big Joe walked slowly, waiting for the dog, whose brutal squared head hung nearly to the ground. Joe Lon watched them limp, the old man and the bloodied dog, across the wide bare yard toward the kennel, where the other pit bulls were growling and barking and snapping at the wire of their individual cages.

The dim light from the television set still showed in his sister's room when he made the turn in his pickup truck to drive toward home.

It wasn't even ten o'clock in the morning and the actual hunt was still nearly forty-eight hours away, but there were already at least a thousand people camped in and around Mystic. They had come in an unrelenting, noisy stream starting long before daylight. Some of them ended up in tents, some bedded down in the backs of pickups, some sat in the open doors of vans, and a great many were in campers of one kind or another. Joe Lon's field was over half full, and spaced neatly along the orderly rows of snake hunters were the white chemical outhouses called Johnny-on-the-spots.

Probably less than half of the people who had arrived were hunters. The rest were tourists of one kind or another, re-tirees stunned with boredom, people genuinely curious about snakes but who had never seen a live one outside a cage, young dopers who wondered about saying gentle, inscrutable things to one another about God, Karma, and Hermann Hesse.

Almost everyone had brought pet snakes to the hunt.

Mostly they were constrictors and black snakes and water snakes. They carried the snakes around with them, passing them from hand to hand, comparing them, describing their habits and disclosing their names.

A surprising number of craftsmen were setting up their wares all over Mystic. Some of the wares were in elaborate booths, pulled in separate trailers, but a lot of things were being sold right off the tailgates of pickup trucks. There were sketches and paintings of snakes, and every imaginable article made from the skin of diamondbacks: cigarette cases, purses, wallets, belts, shoes, and hats. One group of long-hairs was featuring—hanging all over their Volkswagen van—various articles of underclothing, plus several well-crafted items that could only be dildoes of different shapes and sizes; all were marked with the unmistakable pattern of the snake. Several of the dildoes had reshaped and formed rattlesnake heads, complete with fangs. The longhairs had been reported earlier to Sheriff Buddy Matlow by several Senior Citizens, and Buddy, who had been through many of these roundups before and consequently knew that everybody had to be given considerable slack, even longhairs—came by and told them to try not to shock the older folk, that this was all good clean fun, well organized and controlled by himself and his staff and, besides, that it was sponsored by the Greater Mystic Chamber of Commerce, made up mostly of farmers, and therefore had to look after its good name.

Then Buddy bought himself two snake-headed rubbers with diamondback patterns and put them in the glove compartment of his Plymouth patrol car.

But the most spectacular craftsman of all, the one who had the largest audience watching her work and who commanded the biggest prices for the work she did, was an ancient little lady who sat under a white bonnet in a cane-

bottom rocking chair making mosaics out of the individual
rattles from the tails of diamondbacks. There were several
on display; one of them—the largest—about a yard square
was of a buck deer stamping a diamondback to death. It
had taken the rattles from one thousand, one hundred and
sixty-two snakes to complete and the little lady under the
white bonnet who never raised her eyes from the stretched
canvas she was working on in front of her was asking three
thousand dollars for it.

Joe Lon Mackey could see the lady from where he sat
at the little white Formica table in his double-wide drinking
coffee. The crowd around her stood silently in a little semi-
circle as she worked fastening the rattles to the stretched
canvas. She'd been to every roundup as far back as Joe Lon
could remember. And she had always had the three-thousand-dollar mosaic with her.

He suspected she was asking so much because she actually
didn't want to sell it. It was a fantastic thing to see, though,
unbelievable really, with the buck deer, his nostrils flared,
reared onto his back legs, the razorlike front hooves poised
to strike the already cut and mutilated snake on the ground.
And because it was so spectacular, Joe Lon supposed some
sonofabitch would come by sooner or later dumb enough
to pay what she was asking. The world was in short supply
of a lot of things but one of them was not dumb sonofa-
bitches with more money than was good for them.

Joe Lon had gotten up early that morning and gone out,
partly to see if Lummy and his brother George were prop-
erly placing the chemical toilets and partly—mostly—to get
out of the bed and out of the house before he had to face
Elfie.

When he woke up about daylight, the whole sorry business of the night before had risen before his eyes, the
memory of his sister flooding back upon him and his daddy

limping out behind the house with the battered half-ruined bulldog, and then worse, much worse, how it had been afterward when he had got drunker and drunker, remembering that Berenice was coming home, remembering how it used to be with her, thinking about everything the world had promised him and then snatched away until he was stone drunk on the scalding bourbon and drunk on the honey-legged memory of Berenice.

He somehow managed to get what he wished was true confused with the facts of his own life. It wasn't the first time it had ever happened. It was a little quirk his head had of working when he was lost in the sour mist of bourbon whiskey. He had gotten out of his pickup truck in the dark— the moon had gone now, setting behind a black cloud— and gone through the dark, narrow little passageways of the double-wide, stripping his clothes as he went, and fallen finally, savagely, in the bed, not upon his child-ruined wife Elfie but upon the heaving flesh of the University of Georgia's golden head cheerleader, Berenice, or so he thought in the addled disorientation of his alcohol-splattered brain.

But of course it had been poor old Elf, caught unawares and sleeping, her sore flapping breasts vulnerable to his hard square hands. She had come awake with a little muffled cry, protesting, her thin arms trying to push him away, but he had her pinned, driving her against the headboard of the bed. It was a God's wonder he hadn't broken her neck. And when he woke up the next morning he saw her pale face turned off toward the window, her lips partly open, showing her discolored tongue and teeth, the blue smear of a bruise running up from the corner of her mouth, and he knew as the sorry night came back to him in painfully clear memory that he had called her Berenice again and again while he had taken her through the whole routine of enthusiastic sexual gymnastics he and his old high-school sweetheart used to work upon each other's bodies when the world was still a place where such things were not only possible but also a great singing joy in his heart.

There was no joy singing in his heart though when he woke up and realized what he had done, so he had slipped quickly into his Levis, a T-shirt, and a denim jacket, and left the trailer. When he fired up his pickup, he heard both baby boys scream simultaneously. He wondered if something might not ail them younguns, crying the way they did all through the day with such fantastic stamina.

He drove over to the high school first, where they were already building the snake. The cheerleaders, led by Hard Candy Sweet, had sorted out their materials and were starting now to stretch the chicken wire over the frame that eventually would be a papier mâché rattlesnake standing thirty feet high and coiled to strike. That night after the dancing it would explode in one sudden bursting bonfire. Hard Candy was up on a piece of scaffolding and turned to wave to him, but apparently wasn't going to come down to talk to him. He wanted to ask her about Berenice, to ask if she had gotten in from the university yet. Eventually though, watching her bend and stretch there inside her tight red-hot little short shorts (the weather was still holding warm), moving her firm round arms, making her little titties lift and soar, made him impossibly anxious to see Berenice, so he left and drove back to his ten-acre campground, where sure enough Lummy and his brother George had set out the Johnny-on-the-spots in just the neatest and best way, so that he could hardly believe it.

He was standing by the little lady under the white bonnet looking at her thousand-snake masterpiece, admiring the way the deer's hooves showed sharp as razors there above the snake, when Lummy appeared out of the crowd at his elbow.

"Mistuh Joe Lon?"

Joe Lon did not turn to look at him; rather he recognized his voice and kept staring at the fine sharp detail of the rearing deer's hooves. "Everthing's fine," he said. "You and George done a good job gitten them shitters ready."

"Say we done good," said Lummy. "Howsomever, it don be whatall I come to axe you bout."

Joe Lon looked at him for the first time.

"It be Lottie Mae."

"What about her?"

"I want to thanks you for gittin Mistuh Buddy to letter loose."

Joe Lon said: "It's all right. I'as glad to do it."

"Sompin bad wrong with Lottie Mae," said Lummy.

"What ails her?" said Joe Lon, only half listening.

"She be hexed I thinks," said Lummy.

"Hexed?" said Joe Lon, thinking: *Just nigger talk. I spend half my goddam life listening to nigger talk and the other half of it totin whiskey to them. God knows what I did to deserve it.* Believing as he did, though, in the total mystery, power, and majesty of God, Joe Lon assumed he had done *something*, and that he would never find out what it was.

"Mama say she been acting powerful strange since she come in las night," said Lummy.

Joe Lon waved his hand as though brushing away flies. "Look," he said. "You or George one got to stay at the store all day today. I want it kept open to midnight and I want it opened up right now. I ain't gone have no time for the store today."

"I know no Sherf ain't gone hex no gul. Special no nigger gul. Sherf got sompin else to do cept go roun hexin on nigger guls."

Joe Lon blinked. It was as though Lummy had not heard him. And he knew Lummy would go on like that until he took care of Lottie Mae's hex.

"Okay. Right," said Joe Lon. "I'm gone ask Buddy first chance I git. But you right. He ain't hexed nobody, much less Lottie Mae. I'll tell him that being the sheriff, he better see who done it. Is that okay?"

"He ain't gone do that."

"He will if I tell him to."

Lummy gave Joe Lon his blue-gummed smile. "Don think twice. George and me is put our minds on it. Go on and don think twice." He slipped back into the crowd and was gone.

Joe Lon walked around awhile, looking at the booths and speaking to a few people, assuring some of the visitors that, yes, the store would be open tonight, right on until midnight. He saw his old coach, Tump Walker, who was one of the great high-school coaches in the country, and who was Honorary Chairman of the rattlesnake roundup. He was scowling and dripping tobacco juice.

"I tell you, son, they crazier ever year, they are. It's one tourist here that's tainted. If he ain't tainted, I never shit behind two heels. You know what he's got?"

"Whatever it is wouldn't surprise me."

"Surprised me, by God. Sumbitch's got five hundred snakes over there in cages *in* his trailer. Ever kind of snake you could think of's what he's got."

"Why you reckon he's got'm?"

"Beats the shit out of me," Coach Tump said. "Just loves goddam snakes enough, I guess, to go around the country-side in a camper *packed* with'm."

They stood watching each other, thinking about the tainted tourist. Finally, Coach Tump said: "Seen you daddy lately, son?"

"Yes sir, Coach, I seen'm lately. He's fine. How you been?"

Coach Tump sent a long solid stream of tobacco juice into the dirt, shifted the cud in his mouth, hustled his balls and said: "I been real good. But what I thought to ask you was, how's you daddy's Tuff?"

"Trainin real hard, Coach Tump, trainin *real* hard."

"By the good Lord, I allus said, they'd never beat one of you daddy's dogs in the fourth quarter. Aye God, they come to fight."

"Daddy's lookin to retire Tuff. He *knows* he's gone retire Tuff, and then ole Tuff's gone be boss stud of all the pits."

"We all know he will, son."

Joe Lon, always diffident in the face of his old coach and teacher, said: "Listen, Coach, you go on by the store and tell Lummy to give you whatever it is you want. Tell'm to mark it down to me."

Coach Tump said, "You allus was a good boy, son," slapped Joe Lon on the back, sent another stream of juice on the air, and walked away in his rolling bowlegged stride.

Joe Lon was just about to go back to his truck when he saw Berenice all the way across the campground and instantly wanted to run, not sure whether toward her or away from her. He ended by casually strolling in an oblique angle toward the place where she stood with her back half turned to him. But before he was halfway there she tossed her long yellow hair and in the gesture caught sight of him. She went into that high-kneed run, her arms out and smiling, that reminded him of the way she used to run toward him after a game, when he was sweating and bruised and full of victory. He walked a little faster, very self-conscious of the fact that many people there would know who both of them were and how it had been with them before he got down with Elf and the babies and she went on to the University of Georgia, where she was still distinguishing herself with cheerleading and the football team and other achievements.

She threw her arms around his neck and squealed and everything was as it was, the familiar body pressing against him, except that now she seemed fuller, stronger, surer of herself. It was just something he sensed the moment he touched her, something richer and deeper and more complicated. Whatever it was did not make him feel good.

"Joe Lon Mackey! Are you a sight? My, you're just as handsome as ever. My strong handsome beau, and the best football player that ever put on a helmet!"

She kissed his cheek, and he couldn't help thinking that in the old days she would have said: The best football player that ever put on a jockstrap. But these by God weren't the good old days and he hadn't seen her in over a year, because her father, Dr. Sweet, had given her a trip to Paris the previous summer to study French. French! The very notion of somebody studying French threw Joe Lon into a rage.

"You looking good, Berenice. Real good. I got you letter and . . ."

He quit talking because he had gradually become aware of a boy about his own age who had strolled up and was now standing at Berenice's shoulder. The boy leaned forward to look at Joe Lon. Joe Lon disliked him immediately, disliked the soft look of his face, the way his lower lip seemed to pout, and disliked the eyes that would have been beautiful had they belonged to a girl. But it wasn't just the boy's face or the slight, slope-chested way he stood. Joe Lon could have spat on him for the way he was dressed. He'd seen guys dressed like that before and he had never liked one of them: double-knit tangerine trousers, fuzzy bright-yellow sweater, white shoes, and a goddam matching white belt. His hair was neatly cut and looked as though he had slept with his head in a can of Crisco.

Berenice saw him watching the boy and introduced them. "Joe Lon Mackey, this is Shep Martin, from the University of Georgia."

"Shep?" said Joe Lon. Shep was a fucking dog's name, wasn't it?

"Actually, it's Shepherd," said the boy, in a voice that sounded like a radio announcer. "Many men in my family are named Shepherd, my father, an uncle, my grandfather—like that."

"No kidding?" said Joe Lon.

"Shep is on the debating team up at Georgia," said Berenice Sweet.

"Oh," said Joe Lon.

He had never been introduced to anyone on a debating team before and he wasn't sure what to say because he wasn't real sure what it was. Probably some fag foreign game like soccer. Anybody that'd play soccer would suck a dick, that's what Joe Lon thought.

"I've heard a lot about you," said Shep, "what a great athlete you were."

"I played a little football," said Joe Lon shortly, looking off toward the dark fortress-like wall of trees that surrounded his little campground.

"I told you he was modest," said Berenice. "Didn't I tell you he was modest?"

"You sure did," said Shep, "and I just want to shake your hand." He thrust out his hand.

Joe Lon reluctantly took it. "I ain't been on a football field in two years," he said.

For some reason he couldn't meet the boy's eyes. Or even Berenice's. It was all too embarrassing, and that infuriated him. He kept wondering why she had sent him that letter.

Why *had* she sent it?

"How's Elf?" said Berenice.

Joe Lon felt his face get hot. "Okay," he said. "She's okay." He was remembering the pale weak way her thin face looked in the light that morning and the blue smear of a bruise running up from her mouth.

"And the kids? What is it now? Two boys?"

"Yeah, two," said Joe Lon.

"Both of them running backs, I'll wager," said Shep. He leaned forward and actually punched Joe Lon in the shoulder. "Must be great," he said, "just great."

Joe Lon took a step back. He was afraid he was going to snap and coldcock both of them right there. He didn't know what he had been expecting or hoping for from Berenice but it sure as hell was not this.

"Look," he said, "I gotta go."

"Aw," said Berenice, "really? I was hoping you could come over to the house and have a cup of coffee with us."

"Sure, man," said Shep, "I'd like to . . ."—here a little deep-throated radio announcer chuckle—". . . talk some football with you." Now a sudden seriousness about the beautiful girl's eyes. "What do you think about Broadway Joe, anyway?"

"I'd like to talk, but," Joe Lon said, waving his hand to include the campground, the people milling about, the booths where the crafts were being shown, "there's a lot of things I have to take care of."

"But we *will* get together?" said Berenice, taking his arm and squeezing it.

Joe Lon gritted his teeth. "Yeah, we'll get together."

He was turning to go when Shep caught his hand again and pumped it. "It certainly was a pleasure," he said.

Joe Lon mumbled something and walked away between the rows of campers. He walked looking at the ground, feeling that he had somehow just been humiliated. By the time he got to the trailer his jaws were aching from his clamped teeth. Elfie was up and in the kitchen. She was wearing a pretty yellow apron upon which she had embroidered little flowers.

He remembered her working on it when she was pregnant with the second baby. It had ruffles across the top and tended to disguise her ballooning lower belly, for which he was thankful. She had her hair pulled back and tied with a ribbon. And even with the bruise that face powder had not quite been able to cover she looked very cheerful, even happy. He was glad for that because he had not welcomed the thought of facing her after last night.

"You ready for you some breakfast, Joe Lon, honey?" she asked from where she stood doing something at the sink.

"Just coffee," he said.

"Joe Lon, you got to eat, honey."

"Come on, Elf," he said, "I got a little bit of a headache."

"Really?" she said. "You want some aspern?" She hadn't moved from the sink. "I got me some aspern yesterday at the store if you want some."

He held on to the edge of the table and would not let himself say anything. She had already straightened up the trailer and washed and fed the babies. They were both in a playpen by the door in the living room where the sun came through the window. She had done all that and now she was only trying to help him and he knew that and knew also that she could not help it if everything she said drove him wild, nor could she help what had just happened out there to him at the campground. So he just sat at the little white Formica table, holding on to the edge of his chair, and looking out the window. She was watching him and he could feel the weight of her gaze.

"I'll git the coffee, Joe Lon, honey," she finally said.

He nodded but did not answer. His thoughts had already turned back to Berenice and the postcard and the Crisco Kid she had brought home with her. The Crisco Kid, yeah, that's what he was. Second-string lardass on the debate team. Well, Mr. Crisco Kid, it may be you go one on one with Joe Lon Mackey before you get out of Mystic, Georgia. It may be you just got yourself in more shit than you can stir with a stick.

"Honey, here's some fresh hot."

She set the coffee on the table and waited for him to taste it. He bent his head to the raised cup.

"Is it good?"

"Yeah," he said, "it's good, Elf."

She stood where she was, smiling now, but with her mouth conspicuously closed. "You know what, Joe Lon, honey?"

"No, Elf."

"I made me a phone call this morning first thing."

"Okay, Elf."

Through the window he watched the little lady under the white bonnet where she sat unmoving in the bright November sunlight sticking rattles onto a stretched canvas. To the right and in front of her the three-thousand-dollar, thousand-snake deer with the razor hooves kept killing and killing the already mutilated diamondback.

"You know who it was to?" said Elfie.

"No," he said, "I don't know who it was to."

"To the dentist in Tifton." Her voice was rising and lilting, full of surprised triumph. "I called the dentist, and I'm gone git these old sorry teeth of mine fixed."

He turned his eyes from the window to look at her where she had retreated to the sink. He could see now what she was doing. She was washing out baby diapers. Although he had not before, he now smelled the ammonia from his son's piss and he wished he didn't. He forced himself to smile at her as she still watched him over her shoulder.

"That's real good, Elf," he said. "You done real good to do that for youself." His throat felt very tight. "It'll make you feel better."

She left the sink and came to stand behind him. "I done it for you, Joe Lon, honey. I coulda done without it for myself." She moved closer to the back of his chair. Her thin soft hands touched him, one on each shoulder. "Me'n the babies love you, Joe Lon, honey."

He could only nod. He turned loose his coffee and took hold again of the table. He desperately wanted to howl.

Lottie Mae had dreamed of snakes. Snakes that were lumpy with rats. In a dream she killed one of them with a stick and the moment it stopped writhing and was dead, the stick in her hand was a snake. When she tried to turn it loose she saw that she could not because the snake was part of her. Her arm was a snake. And then the other arm was a snake. And her two arms that were snakes crawled about her neck, cold as ice and slick with snake slime.

There were other dreams, but when her mother, Maude, woke her, she could not remember them. But because she could not remember the dreams did not mean she had gotten rid of the snakes. Her mother's hand where it touched her shoulder and gently shook her seemed snaky, the fingers cold with snake skin, and alive with a boneless writhing. She lay as still as stone under the snakes; all that moved was her eyes, which she cut toward her mother bending over her bed only to find the snakes had twisted themselves into the black braids of her mother's hair.

"Chile, I got the miseries," her mother said.

Lottie Mae said nothing but watched the snakes carefully.

"You got to go to Mistuh Big Joe's and do for me."

Lottie Mae drew back the light cover that was over her and got up. Her cotton dress was on the bedpost. She slipped it on and buttoned it up the front.

"Chile," her mother said softly. "Take it off. It got blood on it. I git you sompin else."

But Lottie Mae went into the kitchen instead, where she drank two glasses of water taken with a dipper out of a metal bucket sitting on a shelf. Her mother limped in behind her. The sockets of her mother's hips sometimes fused with the miseries and when this happened the girl had to go to the big house to cook for Big Joe and empty his daughter's slop jar. Her mother came to the water bucket and took her arm. Lottie Mae turned her vacant eyes on her mother. The expression on her face did not change at all.

Her mother smiled but her lips were trembling. "You know chile, Mistuh Big Joe ain't needin you. I spect he be just fine today lak he is. You gone back to bed. I'm gone git Brother Boy to go to the stow and git you some ice cream." The smile jerked on her face and the lips still trembled. "Now how you lak that, chile?"

Lottie Mae seemed to know quite clearly that she could not mention the snakes in her mother's hair or any of the other snakes. She knew it would upset her mother and her mother would not see the snakes and not seeing the snakes would only give her great pain.

"Miss Beeder," said Lottie Mae. She meant to say more and thought that she had, thought that by simply saying the name she had explained what there was to explain about Beeder Mackey.

Her mother took her hand away and said: "Good Lord knows it true. I'm gone git Brother Boy to go with you. You tell Mustuh Big Joe I got the miseries an you gots to come right back home here and hep me. Tell'm you come to do quick an go, cause you cain't stay. Brother Boy can wait right there on the back steps for you."

Brother Boy was her seven-year-old cousin by her Uncle Lummy but the child lived with them because Uncle Lummy and Aunt Lily were bad to fight, fought all the time, had both been cut by razors, each by the other, and drank moonshine whiskey, sometimes separately and sometimes together in the bed, where they were not careful with their nakedness. Maude thought it was sinful and corrupt behavior and had asked for the child. They said she couldn't have him but that she could keep him for a while. James Booker, whom Maude immediately started to call Brother Boy, had walked to their house with a little pasteboard box full of his things to stay awhile. He had been there two years and nobody ever mentioned anything about him going back home.

It took her and Brother Boy, he holding her hand just as Maude had told him to, thirty minutes to walk to Big Joe's house. On the way Lottie Mae saw a long metal truck with rattlesnakes nailed to the sides, she saw a whole parade of people—women, men, and children—carrying pictures of snakes—*signs*—nailed to the tops of wooden standards; then she saw a man get out of the back of a pickup truck with two dead snakes, held by the tail and hanging from each hand like pieces of thick rope. The man was smiling and after he got out of the truck he stood very still while a woman, shrieking with laughter, took his picture.

A boy stood in front of the Mystic grocery store with a snake as big around as her leg and as red as blood draped around his neck. The snake was so long its tail and head both reached the ground. There were people everywhere: in the road, on the side of the road, in the ditches even, beside pickups and cars and buses. They were laughing and talking and shouting to one another and what came to her ears again and again and again from mouths on every side, shouted, said, whispered, sung, was the word: SNAKE SNAKE SNAKE SNAKE SNAKE SNAKE. They were *all* talking about snakes. She half expected the heavens to open up and start sending down snakes. She could feel their thick bodies dropping on her head.

Brother Boy said: "Soda crackers sho am crazy bout snakes, ain't they?"

Her shoulders jerked. "What?" she said.

That word had just come from Brother Boy's mouth and exploded against the side of her head.

Brother Boy said it all again.

She shaded her eyes with her free hand and pretended to squint up the road. "We gots to hurry," she said.

"I wouldn't touch me no snake," Brother Boy said.

"Mistuh Big Joe don't lak it to be late," she said.

"You know they eat them snakes," he said.

"Brother Boy, don't," she said.

He grinned slyly up at her fright and revulsion.

"Every year them soda crackers eat ever snake which they cotch."

She lengthened her stride and turned loose his hand.

"Go in the woods and cotch them snakes," he sang. "Skin them snakes! Skin the skin off and put'm in the fry pan!"

Lottie Mae stopped and turned on him. "Brother Boy!" she screamed. "You got . . . got to . . . got to . . ." She uttered the words until her tongue was hard in her mouth like a single enormous tooth growing out of her throat, because Brother Boy's neck had grown serpentine, undulant under his enormous grinning head.

She turned and ran and Brother Boy chased her all the way to the big house choking on laughter and talking about the white folks' mouths full of squirmy snakes, chewing snakes, swallowing snakes. Right up through the big barren yard to the back porch and up the steps where she slammed the door in his face.

Brother Boy abruptly stopped laughing, went down into the yard, and started throwing stones at a few dusty dirt-scratching chickens under a chinaberry tree that grew out beside the kennel where the killing dogs were kept.

Lottie Mae went to the kitchen and made Big Joe's breakfast: four eggs up, cornbread muffins, ham, and grits. She took it in to him where he was still in bed, propped up in a dirt-colored gown, with a rolled-up woman's stocking pulled onto his head to cover his ears. Propped on the pillow beside him where his wife used to sleep was a bottle of whiskey. When she came in he started shouting.

"Goddammit Maudy, how many times . . ." And then he stopped, staring at her. "Oh, Lottie Mae," he said finally and then repeated several times, "Lottie Mae," in a quiet voice.

Lottie Mae said: "She got the miseries."

While she set the tray beside him on the bed, he rolled the stocking up until his ears were clear.

"What say?" he demanded.

"Miseries," shouted Lottie Mae.

"Lord yes," the old man said. "I guess we all do, ever mother's son of us." He pointed to his bottle and then to his breakfast. "You got to put a bottom on whiskey," he screamed. "Keep a bottom on whiskey and it won't eat you guts out. What daddy used to say. What daddy used to say. Aye God, he'as right too. Food! Food!" he cried and rolled his eyes.

She shouted twice in his good bad ear that she had to go pretty soon, that she didn't mean to stay the whole day, because her mother had the miseries.

"Miseries?" he shouted back. "Lord yes, I guess we all do." As she was leaving he pointed to the wall at the side of his bed where the thumping sound of the television had been shaking an old Currier and Ives print of a bulldog fight. "Don't forgit!" he shouted, his long bony finger trembled at the wall. "Don't forgit! Food, slop jar! Food, slop jar!"

"I'll give her snakes," said Lottie Mae in a quiet voice the old man didn't hear.

"And teller I hope she turns the goddam thing so loud she busts it. Teller that!"

Lottie Mae went out of the room and down the long dark hall to the kitchen. She made up some flapjack batter because Beeder Mackey would not eat eggs or meat. She took the flapjacks and butter and cane syrup and a cup of black coffee into the room where the girl was watching a show on television. A man was trying to give two squealing white ladies a new car, except the two white ladies could not get the answer and it was driving everybody crazy. Lottie Mae put the tray on the bed and Beeder immediately sat up, threw off the blanket, and ate rapidly of the flapjacks and syrup, using her hands and making little grunts of pleasure as she swallowed. Lottie Mae stood at the window while Beeder ate, watching the silvered limbs of the leaf-stripped chinaberry tree under the bright winter sun. Two frightened ruffled chickens came running by, Brother Boy right behind them with a long stick in his hand. He swung the stick rapidly as he ran, narrowly missing the chickens' heads.

Lottie Mae could tell from the sounds behind her that Beeder Mackey had finished.

She turned around and said: "I be afraid it rain snakes."

"Might," said Beeder. "Wouldn't surprise me whatever it was." She pulled the covers tighter around her throat.

"I don't know what to do," said Lottie Mae.

"You know what to do," said Beeder Mackey.

Lottie Mae looked out the window for a long moment,

watching Brother Boy race madly about the yard, hot behind the screaming chickens.

Finally Lottie Mae said: "I misdoubt it."

"Kill it," said Beeder.

"Kill it?"

Beeder smiled her sly sweet smile. "The only way," she said.

"I couldn't kill nothing."

The smile left Beeder's face. "Then find a place to hide."

"Ain't no place to hide."

"No place?" said Beeder. "No place at all?"

Lottie Mae said: "It be the onlyest thing I know. It ain't no place to hide."

"You in trouble," said Beeder. "Bad trouble. It's one thing I can tell you though. Can you shoot a gun?"

"Cain't shoot no gun. Ain't got no gun."

"Knife?" asked Beeder Mackey.

"Razor," said Lottie Mae.

Beeder said: "Don't be without you razor."

"I couldn't kill it," said Lottie Mae.

"Just in case you can, be handy to you razor."

Lottie Mae took the tray and left. She came back shortly and got the slop jar. Beeder watched her carry it carefully out of the room. Directly she brought it back and slipped it under the bed. Neither of them looked at each other and nothing was said. The wild sound of the television filled the room. When Lottie Mae had finally gone Beeder lay very still and watched the little flickering screen where the Wedding Show Game was taking place. The woman wore a white bridal gown and the man at her side a dark suit. The man facing them had an open book in his hand. He was asking them questions. Every time they gave a right answer the audience screamed and another prize—a washer, a radio, a set of silver—was brought in to them.

Beeder lifted her head about an inch off the pillow and strained to hear over the Wedding Show Game, or rather to see if she *could* hear over the Wedding Show Game. A sound came to her that she thought was the sharp deep barking of the pit bulls or maybe it was the mechanical thumping of the electric treadmill on the other side of the wall in her father's room. Whatever it was, it seemed *something* was coming over the sound of the television, so she got off the bed and turned the volume higher, filling her room with the joyous sound of the wedding couple who had just been pronounced man and wife.

Beeder lay back on the pillow, thinking how peaceful everything was, how peaceful *she* was even though they were always trying to trick her. How did they think they could trick her with poor silly Lottie Mae? But they never quit trying and never would quit. She knew that now. But the main thing was that she had found a place every bit as good as her mother's. Sometimes she thought it might be better than her mother's. But most times she did not.

Willard Miller had come by while Joe Lon was still sitting at the little white Formica table in the kitchen. Joe Lon was on about his tenth cup of black coffee, which had revved him up so he had brought out the whiskey and set it beside his cup. Elf was humming contentedly at the baby-smelling sink because after his fourth drink of whiskey he had told her the apron she was wearing was pretty and he wished she'd wear it more.

Willard came in and sat at the table with him and Elf asked if he was hungry and he said yes and Joe Lon said he was ready to eat something now himself so she cooked them both steak and eggs and biscuits. When she had it on the table she asked if she could use the pickup to go to the grocery store. Joe Lon said she could if she took the babies.

"Of course I'm gone take them babies, Joe Lon, honey."

Willard watched the pickup pull away from the trailer and through a mouthful of blood-rare steak he jabbed at the window with his fork and said: "Great little woman," said Willard.

Joe Lon slowly raised his eyes, which were about the color of the egg yolks in his plate and in a dispirited voice said, "You sumbitch."

Willard laughed and wagged his thick blunt head, stopping only long enough to plunge another ragged chunk of beef into his mouth: "I seen Berenice too." He stopped between words to chew and shift the meat with his tongue. "So I . . . goddam know . . . what you studying. Ain't she turned into a world-beatin . . . piece of ass? I wonder if Hard Candy is gonna git super-star titties like Berenice gone off and done?" He winked. "Hard Candy's already gradin out to a eighty-five."

Joe Lon took an egg yolk into his mouth and followed it with a drink of whiskey. "You meet the fag debate player?"

"What?"

"Debate player," Joe Lon said.

Willard smiled and sucked his teeth. "Yeah. Guy on the debate team. I met him. Sweet, ain't he? Looks like a dirt track specialist to me."

The whiskey had now put Joe Lon in a sour mood. At least he guessed it was the whiskey. He belched and regarded Willard. "How the hell you play debate anyhow?"

Willard stopped smiling, looked first serious and then angry. "It'd make you sick just to see it, Joe Lon. They play it with a little rubber ring."

"Rubber ring?" said Joe Lon, feeling an immediate bilious

outrage start to pump from his heart.

"That's what it's played with," said Willard. "These two guys wear little white slippers and . . ."

His voice loud with disbelief and shock, Joe Lon said, "White *slippers*."

"Little pointy fuckers," said Willard. "And they throw the rubber rings to each other and try to catch the rubber ring in their mouth."

Joe Lon stood abruptly from the table. "Mouth?" he yelled. "Mouth!"

"Right'n the teeth," Willard said.

Joe Lon lifted his palm, thick square fingers spread, and stared at it. "Berenice brought that sumbitch all the way to Mystic to shake my hand."

"Looks like it," said Willard.

"Goddam girl's crazy."

"As I remember," said Willard, "she's crazy when she left."

Joe Lon wiped his plate good with a piece of bread. "I wonder what it is she wants?"

"Wouldn't surprise me if it weren't nothing more pressing than a good fucking."

"She's subject to git that," said Joe Lon. "Hell, I'm apt to fuck Shep before it's over."

Beyond the window where they sat, through a haze of dust, campers and pickups roared by and children raced about screaming at one another. Lummy's first cousin, RC, stood at the head of the dim road leading into the campsites, collecting ten dollars a vehicle. He'd grown up with Joe Lon and was going to a junior college over in Tifton. He kept good records, deposited the money in the bank, and never stole more than ten percent, which Joe Lon thought was fair. Besides, they just passed the cost on to the customer.

"Daddy wants you and me to handle Tuffy Saturday

night," said Joe Lon.

"I never thought he'd come to that," Willard said.

"Hearing's got so bad the last few months he ain't got much choice. He don't want to, but he ain't got much choice."

"Hell, I'd be proud to do it."

Joe Lon said: "I'll tell'm."

Willard stood up. "Let's walk out and see what we can see."

Joe Lon followed him to the door. "Just a bunch of crazy people cranking up to git crazier. But that's all right. Feel on the edge of doing something outstanding myself."

"Bring the whiskey."

"I wouldn't leave it."

The campers and tents were arranged in rows on the campground with narrow dusty aisles between them. Willard and Joe Lon walked across the road, stepped over a little dry ditch, and cut up toward the place where RC was taking money and telling people where they could find room to camp.

"It's about twenty more slots and we be full," RC called as they passed.

Joe Lon didn't answer, only nodded. He couldn't get his mind off Berenice bringing Shep all the way from Athens to shake his hand and couldn't keep from wondering if that was all she had done. They walked slowly on between the rows of women starting charcoal fires in grills for hamburgers and men sitting in folding chairs sipping beer, yelling at children who raced mindlessly about with pet snakes. They finally paused in front of a small, badly dented Airstream trailer pulled by a Hudson car. There was a man squatting in the dust at the back of the trailer. They both knew him, or didn't know him really, knew rather only that his name was Victor and that he was a preacher in a snake-handling church somewhere in Virginia. He came to the roundup every year to buy diamondbacks for his church. The congregation of the church never caught its own snakes, but would handle only those caught by strangers. Victor did not look at them when they stopped in front of him. He was wearing overalls and a denim shirt that looked as though he might have slept in them for a long time. His hair was white and full and twisted in tight coils all over his head and down his neck. It was actually Willard Miller who stopped at the Airstream. Joe Lon wanted to go on but Willard stopped and bent to stare into Victor's face.

"Fucked any snakes lately, old man?" The first rush of whiskey always made Willard meaner than usual.

"Don't," said Joe Lon.

Victor cut his eyes at Willard. He looked angry. He always looked angry. Joe Lon had never seen him any other way, like he knew something other people didn't know, and whatever it was he knew was too terrible to say.

"He ain't nothing but a snake fucker," Willard said.

"Don't do that, Willard."

Victor said: "The great dragon was cast out. The old serpent called the devil and satan which deceiveth the whole world. He was cast out into the earth and his angels were cast out with him."

Willard said: "It's not enough shit in the world, we got to have this too."

"Leave him alone," said Joe Lon. "Christ, he's speckled as a guinea hen from rattlesnake bites."

"That's no reason to leave him alone," Willard said.

"Yeah it is. He . . . he . . . Willard, he *believes* all that stuff about the snake and God."

Part Two

Duffy Deeter in an effort of will was thinking of Treblinka. He had already finished with Dachau and Auschwitz. Images of death pumped in his head. Behind his pinched burning eyelids he saw a pile of frozen eyeglasses where they had been torn from the faces of long lines of men, women, and children before they had been led into the gassy showers.

"Daddy. Please, daddy, come. I love . . . love . . . But it hurts."

Duffy allowed his eyes to slide open. He permitted himself one glance through the window of his modified Winnebago. Children raced over the dusting landscape with snakes wrapped about their arms. Directly across the road an old man with twists of gray hair screwed into his head waved his hands wildly at two heavily muscled young men who alternately hustled their balls and spat in the dirt.

Duffy's gaze remained on the two young men for a long moment and then he clamped his eyes shut again. Oh Jesus Oh God. Think about those showerheads and the wonderful gas spewing out into the children. Think about the stunned and naked mothers and their gassed dying children.

Duffy felt her writhe beneath him as she whispered:

"You're killing me."

Yes, and by God he would. He'd kill. He'd do anything.

"You . . . you . . ." She couldn't say whatever it was she was trying to say.

He had her braced against the wall by the bed and he took a steady, resting stroke. He opened his glazing eyes to look through the window again. The old man raised himself from his haunches and walked to the door of his Airstream. He limped. Something was wrong in his hip. He stopped at the door and looked back briefly at the two heavy young men, only one of whom was laughing. A little girl came screaming by with a boy twice her size chasing her with a twisting black snake in his hands.

Duffy closed his eyes again. Under him, Susan Gender was trying to make him look at her. He knew that trick. She'd show him only the deep pink inside her mouth. Make her tongue stand and work like a snake. So he shut out her voice and her body by slipping the garrot around the neck of a fellow prisoner and stealing his half-eaten potato. The prisoner's graspy choking breath mixed with Susan Gender's breath, became her breath. And the prisoner's starving body entered her thrusting thighs and magnificent ass. He killed her where he rode her, there on the high crest of his passion.

"I guess you're too young to remember Pathé News," he said.

They were through now. He was putting on a jockstrap. She lay exhausted on the bed. He had made her cry. But her eyes were dry now and she was staring out the window. He knew she was looking at the two boys across the road, that she had her eyes on the high thrust muscle of their young buttocks rolling under their tight Levis. And he did not care at all.

"Pathé News," she said, her voice numb with exhaustion.

He sat on the edge of the bed and began lacing his blue leather Adidas shoes onto his feet. His eyes were still full of dying children and hopeless parents. "Before television. We used to get the news at the neighborhood movie," he said. "They told us everything. I loved it. One disaster after another. Burning blimps. Collapsing buildings. Ships blowing up."

"It must have been real interesting," she said, getting off the bed. She took an apple from a dish by the window.

She had had gum in her mouth the whole time and her tongue brought it now wetly into her hand. Her white teeth shattered the apple. Little shards of juice flew brightly from her mouth. He watched her in a kind of ecstasy of loathing. He knew her addiction to soap operas on the afternoon TV. And she not only collected science fiction novels, but she also read them. She said they made her think, which meant she was dumb in the gravest kind of way.

"Why don't you go outside," he said, "where everything is going on."

"I don't like snakes," she said.

"You're in a hell of a place if you don't like snakes. Why'd you come?"

"You brought me," she said, getting another apple. "At least I go with you when you take me. That's more than Tish'll do."

It was true. Tish, his wife, wouldn't go anywhere with him. Tish wouldn't go across the street with him if she could help it. Susan Gender, though, would go *anywhere* with him in his modified Winnebago because she was bored witless by her studies at the University of Florida, where she held a Woodrow Wilson Fellowship in the philosophy department. Even so, Duffy thought only something very dumb could eat apples like that. Only the most brutal kind of ignorance could talk the way she did. Duffy couldn't prove it. He just knew it.

"Where you going?"

"A workout," he said.

"Haven't you had enough workout?"

He grinned at her from the door, but there was no humor in it. "I never get enough of anything," he said.

When he went through the door, he and Willard Miller and Joe Lon Mackey came upon one another the way three male dogs might come upon one another at a favorite tree. The recognition was instant and profound. Their eyes met only for a moment, but they did not slide past in a casual glance. Their gazes locked and held for a tense, nearly hostile instant, before rather deliberately they turned their backs on one another.

"What's into that little bowed-up fucker?" said Willard Miller.

"I ain't studying him."

"We both know what you studying," said Willard.

"I think we already talked that to death."

Duffy Deeter came down the steps of his Winnebago with a metal prone press bench in his hands. He went out and set the bench in the sun. He went back into the camper and came out with an Olympic bar and set it on the extended arms of the prone press bench. Joe Lon and Willard watched him casually, without interrupting their conversation about snake hunting and pussy and violence.

Duffy Deeter didn't come back out of the Winnebago right away. Rather, two five-pound plates came flying out and landed in the dirt. Then two ten-pound plates. Then a set of twenty-fives. When the second set of fifty-pounders hit the dirt Willard and Joe Lon hustled their balls, spat, and scowled at each other.

Duffy Deeter came strolling out of the Winnebago wearing only a pair of elastic workout shorts that clung to his rock-like buttocks and swelling thighs like a second skin. Earlier when he'd carried the bar out he'd had on a light cotton sweatshirt and pants and looked like what he was: five-six and about a hundred and fifty-five pounds. Now he looked like he'd said SHAZAM inside the Winnebago, setting off an explosion in his little body so that it was not little any more but roped and strung with incredible muscle.

It was obvious he had warmed up inside. Sweat on his skin shined like oil. He quickly loaded the bar. Across the dusty aisle Joe Lon and Willard watched him. Duffy Deeter regarded the bar, stared at it as though he expected it to maybe attack him. He breathed four quick times, making his rib cage swell like a bellows. On the fourth deep breath he dropped onto his back on the bench, reached up and took the loaded bar out of the cradle, and did ten easy presses, after which he replaced the bar and popped up on his feet. He came up glowering at Joe Lon and Willard. He held them in his feisty little stare.

They ambled across the road toward Duffy Deeter, Willard kicking at little clumps of dirt. He had on his Puma sprinter's shoes this morning. He was closing in on Joe Lon's two-twenty state record and was expected to break it before he graduated. The only record of Joe Lon's he actually owned, although everybody thought he would own them all before the season was over, was Times Carrying The Ball in a single game. Joe Lon's old record had been forty-two. Willard had raised that to forty-five. He had carried the ball every play of the game except three. He told Coach Tump he wanted the record and Coach Tump let him go for it. He took it the first time he had the chance and the Mystic Rattlers still won the game by a margin of twenty-one zip.

Duffy was standing beside the bench breathing when he looked up and pretended to see them for the first time, which both of them accepted as pretense and took no exception to. They would have done the same thing.

"Hey," said Duffy Deeter, grinning, "how you doing?"

Joe Lon smiled back, nodded. Willard said, "We gone be all right."

Duffy Deeter loved young jocks like these who thought they were strong. They always looked as though they had an aluminum cup in their pants and a helmet on their heads. Their universal contempt for anything weaker than they were showed in their faces as a kind of stunned bemusement. And most of them talked as though they had just tackled the goal post with their heads.

"Gittin a little workout?" said Joe Lon.

"Trying to," said Duffy Deeter. "Going to a little iron always makes me feel better."

"Do seem to," said Willard, smiling and winking at Joe Lon, taking no pains to hide the wink from Duffy.

Duffy said: "Jesus, I hate to come off from home like this and have to work out alone." He shook his head. "Hate that."

Willard nodded at the bar. "What you pushing on there anyhow?"

"Two-ten," said Duffy.

Whatever the rush of blood meant that Willard had felt when he first saw Duffy Deeter and the Olympic bar had subsided and he was just about to walk away when the door to the Winnebago opened and a long-legged, black-haired cream-colored piece of ass stood there eating an apple in what may have been the shortest dress Willard Miller had ever seen. Raised the way she was in the doorway, Willard and Joe Lon looked dead into the bulging eye of her pussy. She was wearing red panties.

Joe Lon kept looking at her and said: "I wouldn't mind me a little iron this morning myself."

Willard Miller's eyes never wavered either when he said: "Ain't *nothing* like iron in the morning."

"You're more than welcome to sit in here for a few sets," said Duffy. He enjoyed them looking at the girl. He *liked* them to want her. They wanted her, but by God Duffy Deeter had her.

"It's white of you to say so," Willard said.

"That's Susan Gender up there in the door. My name's Deeter. Duffy Deeter. We came up from Gainesville, Florida."

Both their heads swung slowly to see him grinning at them. They grinned back.

"I'm a graduate student at the University of Florida," said Susan Gender.

Joe Lon thought: Is everbody in college but me? How the hell did I get left out here taking care of chemical shitters and dealing nigger whiskey?

Joe Lon and Willard slipped out of their shirts. Willard flipped over and walked around in the dirt on his hands. Joe Lon took the bottle of whiskey out of his back pocket, set it carefully on the step of the Winnebago, checking out Susan Gender's red pants again as he did. Then he went into a steady handstand and did six dips, his nose just short of the dirt each time he went down. They both came off their hands and looked at Duffy.

"I'm impressed," said Duffy, shortly. "What the hell are you, gymnasts?"

"Drunks," said Joe Lon picking up the bottle.

"I've been known to take a drink myself," said Duffy.

Joe Lon held out the bottle toward him.

"I don't usually drink when I'm working out," said Duffy.

"Why not?" said Willard, taking the bottle out of Joe Lon's hand. "How come you don't drink when you working out?"

"I didn't say I *didn't*. I said I didn't *usually*."

A man came running by with a two-foot black snake, trying to stuff it down the blouse of a screaming woman.

"Nothing much usual about today," said Willard, offering him the bottle again.

"Not a goddam thing that I can see," said Duffy, taking it. He took a long pull at it while he watched Joe Lon do the first set of warm-up presses on the bench. They talked and warmed up, casually adding weight between sets.

A little man came around the corner just as Duffy was getting off the bench. His hair was gray and he was color-coordinated in brown plaid slacks, a beige Banlon shirt with crossed golf clubs over the heart, and a ventilated golfing cap. A paunch, round and mobile as a ball, rode under his belt. He stopped and said almost shyly: "I've been looking everywhere for you."

"You've been looking for *me*?" said Duffy Deeter.

The little man smiled and looked just over their heads at the distant horizon. "Well, you're the only one I know here and . . ."

Joe Lon came over and laid his big square hand on the back of the little man's neck and offered him the whiskey bottle. "Why don't you have a drink and git out of the way? You fucking up the workout."

"I'm sorry. I didn't know . . ."

"It's all right," said Willard. "Now you know." He turned a short hard glance toward Joe Lon and then back to the little man. "Say, you ain't a salesman are you? A traveling salesman? You look like you might be one to me."

Joe Lon closed his hand on the neck he was holding. Closed in hard. "What?" he said. "You cain't be a fucking salesman. It ain't allowed."

They were both leaning in on him now, one on each side. The workout, the sweat, the whiskey, and the sight of

Susan Gender's red underwear had made them feel good. They were playing. But the little man didn't know that. They looked as though they were set to go crazy mean.

"What you saying?" the little man cried, sucking desperately at the spit spinning between his lips. He stared wildly at Duffy Deeter. "Tell'm who I am. Tell'm I'm Enrique Gomez." He glanced up at Willard, who regarded him with a kind of objective, passionless malevolency. "My friends call me Poncy. Poncy!"

Willard Miller looked at Joe Lon. "What kind of name is Eniquer Gomez?"

Joe Lon said: "It ain't our kind of people, is it?"

Duffy Deeter was smiling. Up in the door, Susan Gender was smiling. Willard and Joe Lon each had one of Poncy's arms. They were even smiling now, but to Poncy their smiles looked terrible.

Poncy said: "My friends call me Poncy. Honest to God they really do call me Poncy."

Duffy Deeter said: "He told us that on the road, last night."

"That's what he told us," said Susan Gender. "We met'm at the Magnolia Truck and Rest Stop coming into town and that's what he told us."

Joe Lon seemed to grow hot, to burn all along his veins. He looked at Willard with genuine puzzlement. "I'm damned if I know what to do about this."

Duffy Deeter sat down on the bench, smiling, gazing with great fondness upon the bulging mound of Susan Gender's blender, as he called it in moments when he felt good. Listening to these country boys playing with the old man pleased him. It amused.

They kept Poncy lifted on his toes while he frantically explained that he was born in Cuba, brought to Tampa at the age of five, and educated at the University of Florida.

Here he started an addled singing of the University of Florida's Alma Mater, with Susan Gender screaming in the background that he fucking-A-well had the words right. *That was it.* He stopped singing and was rapidly talking about his life's work in bananas when Hard Candy Sweet appeared between two tents across the road.

She came straight to them and said, "What you two assholes doing to this little sapsucker?"

"We was gone kill him," said Willard, smiling. "But I think we'll just leave him alone and let him bore his goddam self to death."

They let him down on his heels. Joe Lon straightened Poncy's shirt, smoothed his collar. Then he raised Poncy's chin with the end of his little finger and looked directly into Poncy's eyes. "But you ain't no traveling salesman, are you?"

"No. No sir! Retired. I'm re . . ."

"You didn't retire from being no salesman neither, did you?"

That was precisely what Poncy's specialty had been. And he had risen to Director of Sales for all of bananas before he was through.

But he saw that was not the right answer. "Engineering," said Poncy. "I was an engineer."

Joe Lon gave him a thin whiskey smile. "Got a uncle that was a railroad man."

Willard had introduced Hard Candy to Susan Gender and it turned out Susan had been an undergraduate head majorette herself back at Auburn University in Alabama and they went down and lined up hip to hip on the grass at the end of the trailer working on a little routine.

"Now after the first kickout, you spin and do a split," said Hard Candy Sweet. Her little eyes shined. "Can you still split?"

"Lord yes, honey," said Susan Gender. "I'm still just limber as a dishrag."

Willard was on his back on the bench pumping two hundred and fifty pounds. Poncy was whispering, "Are they crazy, or what?"

Duffy didn't answer right away; he only looked at Poncy. Finally he said: "You better get over there out of the way."

Joe Lon and Willard slid a ten-pound plate on each end of the Olympic bar.

"You set," said Joe Lon.

Poncy walked over and did not so much sit as collapse onto a little grassy bank of dirt.

The girls came high-kicking by and Susan Gender sang: "We're going inside." She stopped in the door and called: "You want anything, Duffy?"

Duffy, who was in the middle of a press, did not answer, but Joe Lon Mackey, beginning to buzz from the whiskey, feeling better than ever in the old familiar demand of muscle and sweat, said: "Got any bourbon whiskey up there in that trailer?"

Susan Gender gave a little kick and laid the full weight of her smile and single red eye upon him. "Duffy Deeter wouldn't go anywhere without it."

"You might just bring us out a bottle," Joe Lon said.

"If you got any of them cold beers in there," said Willard Miller, "bring a few. Damned if that straight corn ain't beginning to burn my breakfast."

"Pussy," said Joe Lon.

"You better hope so," Willard said. "Slip on that other ten."

They were doing only three repetitions on the bench now, and they were no longer adding weight casually but slamming it on with little grunts of challenge and pleasure.

When they went through the door of the Winnebago,

Hard Candy looked up and said: "Hey, those are great trophies."

There were trophies mounted along three walls, bracketed and gleaming on specially constructed shelves.

"You oughta see them two guys' football trophies out there. Knock you eyes out. They're stars, you know."

"Duff said he wouldn't ever have anything to do with a team sport. He always said somebody else could just have the team sports."

Although Hard Candy knew there were trophies for other sports—didn't Willard have a shelf full from track?—nobody she knew thought a trophy was a real trophy unless it was from football.

"What are all them from?" said Hard Candy.

"Karate mostly. Some from handball. Duff was the state singles champion in handball for four years. That right there is something the ABA, you know, the American Bar Association, gave him for coming in fifteenth in the Boston Marathon."

Hard Candy could only blink at the trophies. A lawyer that played handball? Willard was apt to kill him and eat him.

Susan Gender smiled at her. "I know what you're thinking. That's what I thought at first. But don't be fooled, that little bastard out there is dangerous."

Poncy came bursting through the door, his face ash-gray under his Cuban color. "They said I better get the whiskey and beer," he said rapidly. "They said I better."

"Jesus," said Susan, "I forgot."

She got the bottle out of a cabinet and the six-pack of tallboys out of the refrigerator. Poncy rushed outside with it in his arms.

"That old man ought to git away from them boys," said Hard Candy, "him being like he is and all. One of'm git drunk enough and git to feeling mean, and I don't know."

They had gradually moved to a window while they talked and they stood now watching the three of them take turns pressing off their backs. Duffy was on the bench and Willard and Joe Lon were on either side, leaning forward yelling at him as he strained to finish the press, yelling in short, abrupt phrases. Veins stood in their necks and their heads jerked as if they might have been barking. Poncy sat on the little bank of dirt, alternately clapping his hands the way the boys were doing and looking afraid. Dust rose around the bench and clung to their sweating bodies. They didn't seem to see it.

Big Joe Mackey limped through the hallway of his house toward the kitchen. It was only a little after noon but here inside the high-ceilinged old house the shadows were deep in the corners and along the warped walls. He stopped at his daughter's door and leaned against it listening. He heard what he had been hearing all day, the mad babble of the television set. Lottie Mae had finished and left and he knew he could not depend on her to come back; he would probably end up having to cook his own dinner, but he didn't mind too much because Lummy had brought over another bottle of whiskey and he'd do his cooking in a mild red drunken mist. Beeder wouldn't get anything else to eat until tomorrow when the cook came.

He leaned his head against the door and called: "You all right in there, youngan?"

For answer he got a sudden booming of the television as the volume was turned up. He'd be damned if he would go in there. She was well enough to hop out of bed and turn up the sound. That was good enough for him. He hadn't raised his daughter to be crazy, goddammit. But she'd always been a headstrong girl and if she wanted to be crazy the rest of her life, that was her little red wagon and she'd have to pull it. He wasn't going in there to see her craziness and see . . . see . . .

There his mind stopped. He quit thinking, and his daughter's face gradually emerged out of the red mist of his eyes, Beeder's face, which was only the younger uncracked copy of his wife's face. He stood, suddenly shaken, saying quietly: "Damn them all. Damn them all." But try as he would to keep it from happening, he saw all over again his wife sitting in her favorite rocker with the bag over her head.

He went into the kitchen and got the dog bucket. It was a five-gallon bucket and he filled it nearly full with canned meat and double-yolk eggs. Then he stirred in ten ounces of a special vitamin mixture he made up himself. He limped awkwardly with the bucket down the back steps and out across the bare dirt yard to the kennel. The kennel was a long narrow concrete slab with individual wire cages fastened to the top of it. There were four puppies, not quite three months old. They were solid red and already broad-chested and thick-necked, standing on their hind legs barking happily at the sight of the bucket. The two dogs next to the puppies were grown but had not yet started their hard training. The only thing they did was a little game that all the pit bulls loved. He had an old rubber tire tied to the end of a rope hanging from an oak tree behind the kennel. These two young dogs, approaching fighting age, were allowed to swing from the tire an hour a day three days a week. He would rub the tire with a little blood—chicken blood—and take the dogs out one at a time to the tire, set it swinging, and turn them loose. They would leap and set their massive jaws to the tire and swing, their thick little bodies drawn up tight and tucked into a solid muscular ball. Big Joe thought that next month he would muzzle both of them and put them in together to see how they faced off. Sometimes a strain weakened and played out for no reason at all. The dog would look great but at the center of him would be a soft rotten spot of something that made him go bad.

He fed the puppies, who never stopped yelping until he dumped big hunks of meat and egg into their troughs. The dogs next to the puppies—their brothers—barked too, but it was a slower, deeper bark, and their steady red-eyed gaze was more serenely and savagely sullen. They stood in solid, slightly bowlegged dignity at their troughs swallowing heavy chunks of food each time their great heads jerked. Their bony skulls were insistent under their fine tight skin. Tuffy was next in the line of cages and he did not bark at all. He had rounded into condition beautifully. No matter how badly you hurt him, he came back steady and strong after a single day's rest. His wounds had scabbed nicely. Tuffy turned slowly and looked down the row of cages at his noisy sons and seemed to see them and dismiss them at the same time with a fine contempt. Big Joe watered Tuffy but did not feed him.

In the end cage, which was slightly larger than the others, was Tuffy's daddy, also named Tuffy. He'd won six fights before he was retired to stud and became the top of the line; his blood was in every fighting animal Big Joe owned, including the two ferocious bitches housed on the reverse side of the kennel where the males could not see them.

Old Tuffy, as he was called to distinguish him from Tuffy the Younger, had thickened in his old age. A coarse gray ruff grew round his neck and he was nearly blind. He had not mated in a long time. His fine razor teeth had been worn down to dull yellow stubs in his mouth, a mouth that once closed like a steel trap but that now was wet and a little slack, a little jowly like an old man's. Like his son in the cage next to him he did not bark or even growl but stood with the magnificent balance he still had even in old age, watching Big Joe with solemn faded eyes held in a net of red veins as Big Joe limped by with the meat bucket. Big Joe watered him with the running garden hose lying on the edge of the concrete slab, but did not feed him. He clucked to the old dog and spoke to him in a soft, rough, but gentle voice. Then he went around on the other side of the kennel and fed and watered the bitches. When he was done with the bitches, he came back to the old dog's cage, and with a key off a ring on his belt, he opened the padlock on the steel U-neck that formed the latch. He swung back the heavy wire gate.

The old pit bull walked out of his cage and stood blinking in the thin sunlight. He shook himself and bent his head to lick his muscled forepaw with a tongue wide as a man's hands. Big Joe knelt stiffly beside him.

"You ole sumbitch," said Big Joe in a whisper at the dog's head. "You done got too old to fight. An you done got too old to fuck." He scratched and rubbed the gray ruff at the dog's thick neck. "You had you goddam day in the ring though. You done what you done as good as any dog that ever come down the pike. Wisht I had a nickel on the dollar for ever bet passed over you back." Big Joe sighed and looked at the cage where Tuffy regarded them both, standing four square to his wire gate, a slow but insistent growl rattling wetly in his throat. "Yessir," said the old man vaguely. "True, ever bit of it true. But you done got too old to fight. And you done got too old to fuck."

He got slowly to his feet and took a steel muzzle off a rack hanging on the cage. The old dog did not resist the muzzle and when he had it securely in place, Big Joe put a steel choke collar on him and fastened the collar to a short leather strap that was in turn tied to a short metal post. Then he opened Tuffy's gate and got down on his knees and muzzled him while he was still in the cage. He was trying to get a leather lead fastened to his choke collar when Tuffy burst past him and seemingly did not touch the ground again until he landed on his daddy still tied securely to the metal post. The growls coming from the two dogs as they rolled together on the ground was like an electric saw cutting through something soft but now and then hitting something hard and resistant. Big Joe got slowly to his feet cursing softly but good-naturedly and limped over carefully to the snarling, clawing dogs. He got Tuffy by the tail and dragged him clear of the reach of the leather lead fastened to the post. He hit him on the top of the skull with his fist to calm him down and then got a leather strap attached to his choke collar.

With a muzzled dog on a short lead in either hand he stared off toward a place about fifty yards away where wooden bleachers formed a square. The bleachers rose maybe twenty-five feet high and enclosed a square hole in the ground three feet deep and twelve feet across. The sides of the hole were reinforced with close-driven wooden stakes but the bottom was only hard-packed earth. A set of portable wooden steps led down into the hole. As Big Joe went through the gate of the fence and the dogs saw the hole, they immediately bowed, started walking stiff-legged. The hair rose along the indentation of their heavily muscled backs. They lunged against their short leads trying to square off to each other. Big Joe kicked them both in the ribs with his thick brogan shoe and spoke to them in a quiet, good-natured voice.

"You dogs," he said. "You dogs stand easy."

He wished he had thought to bring his whiskey. He didn't particularly dislike this, but there was no pleasure in it either. It was simply necessary, like feeding a young savage boxer a lot of inferior opponents, opponents who had some skill but no chance, no real hope. It tuned the fighter, gave him a taste for blood and the killing blow, made him feel invincible. Big Joe had saved the old dog for this final sharpening of the son and future stud of the line. It never occurred to him to wish that it did not have to end this way. It always had to end this way and he had always known it.

He went carefully down the steps into the pit. Both dogs followed him down, but by now they were so excited that they closed at the top step and came into the pit locked together, their steel muzzles grinding. Big Joe watched dispassionately as the two dogs parted briefly, standing in the center of the pit now, heads together, their short wide bodies braced and waiting. Their eyes were locked and they balanced each other in a bright and ferociously insane stare.

Big Joe wondered, as he had more than once when dogs were about to stand to one another, what might be going on in their heads. Could dogs think? What were they thinking? Probably nothing. They weren't men; they didn't think; they fought.

There was a steel hook built into the wall on each side of the pit. He separated the dogs and fastened their leads to the hooks. Then he removed their muzzles, first slapping them hard twice with his heavy square-fingered hand to get their attention so they didn't accidentally crush a finger or a wrist in their fighting frenzy. Once their muzzles were off Big Joe moved to release them, but Tuffy broke his lead and was across the pit and on his daddy in a blinding move full of slashing teeth and roiling dust and flying shards of bright slobber. The dog's body, catapulting across the pit, had struck Big Joe on the shoulder where he had been kneeling beside Old Tuffy and knocked him halfway across the circle. He got up slowly and sat on the reinforced wall. Old Tuffy would not have had much of a chance anyway but fastened

on the lead as he was made it a shorter fight than it otherwise would have been. It wasn't more than forty-five seconds
before Big Joe could see that he was already taking a killing.
Tuffy was into his throat. The sound of blood was in his
breathing as Tuffy settled in deeper and shook him now like
a toy. Big Joe let Tuffy stay on as long as he liked, letting
him chew his fill, until at last Tuffy backed off, gazed quietly
and somberly at the slashed and bleeding body, and then
trotted happily across the pit to his master.

Big Joe was deeply satisfied at the way Tuffy had peaked
into condition. He'd feed him now, rest him good, and by
fight time tomorrow night he would be as ready and savage
as he had ever been. He led Tuffy back and put him in his
cage. For a long time then he stood staring at the two grown
bulls in the next cage. Finally, he chose one of them, put
him on a leash, and led him back up to the house.

They had fought each other to an absolute draw
on the bench, but they both knew that one of them would
have lost if Duffy Deeter had not run out of weights. And
neither of them was dead solid certain which of them it
would have been. Duffy Deeter had gone with them up to
an even three hundred pounds, which astounded them both
and immediately changed their attitude toward him.

A hundred-and-fifty-pound guy who could get three hundred pounds on the bench was nobody to fuck with. It
meant that somewhere there inside him was a little knot of
craziness that made him pay the price. But it was not entirely enough to make them forgive him for weighing a
hundred and fifty pounds. He was still a runty, second-
string grunion. But a very *strong* grunion.

They'd left him at three hundred and then both got one final rep with three-twenty, which was all the weight Duffy had with him in the Winnebago. Joe Lon and Willard were fired up and when they found out there was no more weight they automatically faced off and almost went one on one against each other right there in the dirt and probably would have if it had not been for Susan Gender. Duffy Deeter had enjoyed it immensely and was hoping they might hurt each other, because while he admired them for turning out to *be* stud jocks instead of just looking like they might be, he could not forgive them for beating him. He wasn't used to getting beat, even by men who outweighed him fifty or sixty pounds. So it was left for Susan Gender to stop them. She had been watching through the window with Hard Candy Sweet when Willard popped up off the bench and turned to face Joe Lon, whose response was to dip slightly, bring his elbows out from his body, and thrust out his thick corded neck.

"He's gone strike a lick," Hard Candy said happily.

"What? Which one?" said Susan Gender.

"Take you pick," said Hard Candy. "They fixin to bust ass."

But Susan got to the door first and cried: "Let's go find us a tonk!"

Duffy and Poncy looked at her but Joe Lon and Willard only slightly shifted their bodies toward her, the smallest change in the position of their shoulders. But their eyes stayed locked on each other.

"Tonk," said Willard quietly, not a question, just repeating the word.

"I want to dance!" cried Susan Gender. "I want to play the juke and eat a pickled pig's foot. I want to drink beer and *shake my ass*."

Now they turned together to look at her and stared with

hostility at her head majorette legs straddling across the door frame.

"Ain't no tonk in this county," Joe Lon said. "It's damn nigh fifteen miles."

"Shit, boy," said Susan Gender. "We got wheels." She spread her arms and looked back into the Winnebago. "Duffy Deeter ain't got nothing if he ain't got wheels."

Poncy, suddenly alive again in their young contentious voices, said: "I got a Porsche my own sef," and two things happened at once. First, Poncy was sorry he had opened his mouth about his sweet expensive Porsche car, and second everything got very quiet and still while they stared at him. He had not meant anything by imitating, or trying to imitate, their grit voices. He'd only been trying to be one of the group. But he could see in their faces they had heard what he said as mockery. He tried to explain what he really meant but they wouldn't hear it. Joe Lon and Willard each got an arm and led him protesting down the dirt street to where his car was parked.

"Hard Candy," Joe Lon called over his shoulder. "Go with them, show Deeter. Blue Pines."

"But I spose we gone already be drunk a beer by the time you git there in that Winnebago," called Willard, "cause this sucker's got a Porschie and I hear them things won't do nothing but fly."

They put Poncy in the back seat of his own Porsche and Joe Lon drove. The country was flat but the road was winding and Joe Lon one-handed the car through one tight turn after another, not bothering to use the gears but keeping it flat out with Poncy first outraged and then terrified in the back seat. Halfway there, Willard puked out the window, not much but enough for some of it to blow into the back seat where Poncy was trying to duck. Willard did it as easily as spitting. The stream slipped from between his lips, he blinked twice, and wiped his mouth with his hand.

He looked over at Joe Lon. "Musta been that fucking meat we et at breakfast," he said.

Joe Lon handed him the bourbon. He took a mouthful, gargled, spat it through the window, and then drank long from the bottle, his powerful throat pumping and pumping. When he finished he turned and tried to hand it to Poncy, who had been watching the whole thing from his place crouched in the back. "Want you own *sef* a drink a whiskey?" said Willard.

At that moment Joe Lon was taking the Porsche through a long slow curve in a power slide that was turning a hundred and ten. Joe Lon was screaming, not with joy, not with anger, just screaming, his thick fine hands locked on the steering wheel. Poncy saw a huge oak tree tilting into their line of vision at the top of the curve and smelled the raw bits of puke clinging to his Banlon shirt and saw the offered whiskey bottle sloshing just there in front of his eyes and although he knew what he was going to do—could not help doing—he bowed his head and puked onto his lap while Willard Miller sucked his teeth and watched dispassionately from the front seat.

Willard said: "This sumbitch in the back seat just thrown up on his self."

But Joe Lon didn't hear. He was on a long straight and he had the Porsche up to a hundred and twenty, which was apparently all it would do because he was stamping the accelerator and pumping the steering wheel with both hands. He glanced over at Willard and shouted: "Ain't had a chance to drive nothing like this since Berenice went off to the U of Gee and given her Vette to Hard Candy!"

Joe Lon drew his lips back in what could have been great happiness, but it was not. Even in the middle of this frantic ride, with his best buddy sitting beside him screaming for him to *Screw it on*! he felt the weight of a great despair settling in him as solid as bone. It had started in the middle of the workout on the prone press bench and he was not even aware of it until it was on him like a fever. He had gotten up from the bench and, waiting for Duffy and Willard, found himself looking across the road at the old man who had come back and squatted by the end of his Airstream trailer. The twisting tufts of hair stood out like something driven into his skull and across his knees was an open book that he was reading, his finger tracing and tracing the page as he read.

It was a long time before Victor shifted the book and Joe Lon saw it was the Bible. Victor used to take a room on the second floor of their house back in the days when Big Joe used to let rooms to tourists and hunters for the Roundup. Victor never talked of anything but God and snakes and his voice and the look in his eyes always made Joe Lon's heart jump. His daddy, who had been to meetings at Victor's church, had told Joe Lon how it was.

"He strings diamondbacks in his hair like a lady strings ribbons. I seen'm kiss a snake and a snake kiss him. He's been bit in the mouth. He's been bit everwhere. It ain't no more'n a kiss from his ma. He follers where God leads him."

It was Joe Lon's turn on the bench and he went under the weight in a sinking despair, thinking: *What am I doing here on my back? What is this I'm doing? I'm a grown man with two babies and a wife and I'm out here fucking around with weights. What the hell ails me?*

When Joe Lon got off the bench the next time, Elizabeth Lilly Well—called Mother Well by the hunters, who gave her buttons from the tails of rattlers—was sitting on a stone beside Victor. She had brought her three-thousand-dollar mosaic called *Deer Plus Snake* with her. It gleamed in the sun and Victor traced its outline with one bony finger. It came to Joe Lon that she pinned rattles to a canvas relent-lessly and with great joy and Victor followed God the same way. What did he, Joe Lon, do? What did he have? He had once had football to fill up his mind and his body and his days and so he had never thought about it. Then one day football was gone and it took everything with it. He kept thinking something else would surely take its place but nothing ever did. He stumbled from one thing to the next thing. From wife to babies to making a place for crazy campers bent on catching snakes. But nothing gave him anything back. So here he was lying under a dead weight doing what he'd done five years ago, when he was a boy. If it had meant anything then, he had forgotten what; and merciful God, it meant nothing now. His life had become a not very interesting movie that he seemed condemned to see over and over again.

"I feel like the end of the world," Joe Lon screamed above the noise of the whining engine.

"We git up here," Willard screamed back at him, "we'll press a little beer to you face, you'll feel better."

But he would not feel any better and he knew it.

Poncy, sitting with the little green puddle in his lap, tried to say something authoritative to them about abusing his car, after all he *was* old enough to be their father and there was no reason for him to take all this and not let them know what they were in for if they wrecked his Porsche or hurt him. But they either did not hear him yelling up at them from the back seat or they simply did not care.

They roared into a clay parking lot and stopped. Joe Lon and Willard got out and closed their doors without ever looking at him. He sat where he was and watched them walk away. His bowels felt loose. He'd been having a lot of trouble with his bowels since he retired, and the ride had not helped. When he was sure he had everything under control, he got out. In the red clay parking lot he shifted quickly from foot to foot, testing the weight of his bowels. Everything seemed to be all right.

The Blue Pines was a wooden building with a tin roof. Various signs were stuck on the walls advertising Budweiser, the King of Beers, and Redman chewing tobacco, and Coca-Cola, pool table, and sandwiches. The hills sloped away in thin, second-growth pine trees. When Poncy opened the door it was so dark he had to stand a moment before he saw Willard and Joe Lon sitting at a round splintered wooden table and another man bringing a pitcher of beer with two glasses.

The man said: "You boys welcome here, but I don't want no goddam trouble." He set the pitcher on the table.

Neither Joe Lon nor Willard looked at the man. They poured beer into the glasses and drank. The man stood beside the table. Finally, Willard—still without looking up —said: "Pay'm, would you, Conty?"

"Poncy," said Poncy, paying the bartender, "it's *Poncy*."

The man stood beside the table with the money in his hand and said: "How's you daddy's Tuffy?"

"Tuffy's good. Great shape," said Joe Lon.

"He's old, though," said the man.

"You put anything down, better be on Tuff," Joe Lon said.

"Knowing when to git off a dog is smart as when to git on."

"Suit youself."

There was only one other man in the Blue Pines, a farmer in overalls and felt hat, drinking whiskey out of a water glass and never looking up. Willard and Joe Lon managed to get through two pitchers of beer before the Winnebago pulled in. Duffy Deeter drank straight from the pitcher to catch up and then proceeded to take Joe Lon and Willard to the pool table in back and humiliate them. During one run he went through two consecutive racks, which did not improve Willard's humor.

Susan Gender put two quarters in the juke for six plays. She stood prancing on her toes in front of the jukebox for a moment and then cut her sly gaze at Poncy, where he stood trying to act as though he wasn't watching her pumping hips and the fine vibrating flesh of her belly.

She smiled. "I guess you it," she said, and came dancing toward him.

"No, wait!" he said, as she pulled him toward the floor. I slept in the car last night, my back . . ."

"All the more reason to shake youself loose," she said.

She held his hand and whipped her hard lean body through the Dog and the Frug and the Pony and the Swim. As Hard Candy crossed the dance floor for more beer, she pinched Poncy's old flabby ass. He tried to turn around but Susan Gender held his hands tight.

"Please," said Poncy, but a little jolt of pleasure had moved on his spine.

"I'm gone give you a goose ever time I catch you not shaking it," yelled Hard Candy Sweet.

Poncy saw the farmer slowly lift his eyes under the brim of the felt hat and look at them steadily, with no expression at all on his face. His eyes looked like nailheads over his wind-burned cheeks. Poncy started moving his hips and shoulders and hands. He had no idea if what he was doing was right. There did not seem to be a right or wrong way, since Susan Gender wasn't doing anything the same way twice.

Joe Lon and Willard came wandering over from the pool table to the dance floor. Behind them Duffy Deeter still leaned on the green velvet table under the swinging overhead light.

"Come on back over here," he called.

"What did he win off you?" Hard Candy asked.

"Couple dollars," said Joe Lon.

"You could train a goddam monkey to shoot pool," Willard said.

They stood at the edge of the dance floor watching Poncy jump awkwardly about, hobbling after the spinning, stroking Susan Gender.

"Susan's teaching Poncy to dance," Hard Candy said. "Ain't he just the ugliest fucking thing you ever seen?"

"Well, shit," said Joe Lon, "if Enreeker wants to dance, we'll hep'm. Git us another pitcher, Hard Candy."

Joe Lon walked out onto the floor. Willard turned a chair around, sat down, and put his arms on the back of it. Hard Candy went to the bar for a pitcher and stood looking at Willard while it was drawn from the tap. Joe Lon stopped alongside Poncy and Susan. Poncy was concentrating on his broken little dance when Joe Lon picked him off his feet. He caught Poncy's belt on each hip and lifted him as if he'd been a child. Poncy's feet kept moving while Joe Lon turned him through the air and set him down in front of Willard's chair.

"We don't allow nothing half-ass around here, Enreeker," said Joe Lon bitterly. "You gone dance, goddammit, you got to *dance*."

Hard Candy came back with the beer. Duffy Deeter had strolled out onto the rough wooden floor in front of the jukebox and pumped in some more quarters. Susan Gender had sweated through her blouse and the farmer's nailhead eyes watched her little hard-nosed titties plunge against the fabric as she jacked around to the music while James Brown screamed: "I don't know karate but I know kaRAZOR."

"I had to sleep in the car last night," Poncy was trying to say. "My back hurts like a . . . like a . . ." But he couldn't get it out because Joe Lon had him by the seat of the pants and Willard had him by the belt buckle and they were punching his hips back and forth between them.

"Basic move," shouted Joe Lon right into Poncy's face. "It's you stroke. You cain't stroke, you cain't dance."

"Oh, God, God," said Poncy, his eyes round, his lips gray. They were hurting him. But if either of them knew it they didn't show it. Their own faces were flushed, their lips peeled back in what was alternately snarl and laughter.

"Watch *her*," cried Willard, still seated, still holding Poncy by his double knits, punching him in the ass counterpoint to the punch Joe Lon gave him in his old melon belly. Poncy was beginning to hunch and stroke as best he could to avoid being hurt but he couldn't do it very well because there was a stick of pure fire standing in his lower back. He was terrified that he would either cry or shit on himself. The punches in the belly had made him flatulent but thank God, *thank God* the music was loud enough to cover him. "Watch *her*," Willard was screaming in his ear.

"Wave you goddam hands, Enreeker," said Joe Lon.

Poncy waved his hands.

"Watch'r feet," said Joe Lon.

Poncy could only roll his eyes at them and wave his hands and arms.

Duffy had been leaning against the slot, where he was feeding quarters into the jukebox. His eyes and Willard's happened to meet briefly and when they did Duffy came bucking across the floor to Hard Candy. His hands moved in one direction, his feet in another, his body in still another, all of it synchronized with the music and all of it at blinding speed. His head stayed rock still, his eyes fixed on Hard Candy. She'd stopped pouring beer and set the pitcher down. Her eyes were shiny, her lips swollen. Her body started to pulse, then pump, and they moved out onto the dance floor, separate, no longer even looking at each other, but absolutely together.

"Jesus," said Willard to Joe Lon, "ain't it nothing that little sucker cain't do?"

They held Poncy tight between them, and since they had stopped making him hunch and flap his arms he thought they were through with him. He took a deep breath and just to keep things nice and easy and conversational so they wouldn't think of punching him again, Poncy said: "He's quite something, isn't he?" He'd made it as formal as he could because he didn't ever want them to think he was mocking the way they talked again, but Joe Lon turned on him anyway, jerking as if he had been burned. His nostrils flared. His head seemed to tremble, and his staring blue eyes were intense enough to look crossed.

"Quite something?" Joe Lon demanded. "Willard, is he gone stand around saying shit like *quite something* or not?"

Willard popped out of his chair, raising Poncy about six inches off the floor by the belt when he did. Poncy got one quick glimpse and closed his eyes. Willard looked completely nuts. Willard and Joe Lon, shouting *quite something, quite quite something*, dragged Poncy toward the center of the dance floor. Once they had him out in front of the jukebox, each of them took one of his hands and started going round and round him as if he was a maypole and each of his arms were streamers. They held tight and skipped in a little dance step to the music. Hard Candy stopped dancing and took hold of Poncy too. Hard Candy had him by the tail of his Banlon shirt and Susan Gender, unable to find anything better to hold on to, caught Poncy by a roll of fat on his hip. They were laughing and singing and Poncy was screaming but the music was so loud it sounded like they were all having just the best time. Poncy was very dizzy and very sick to his stomach and a thin

stream of shit had slipped down his leg. He tried to fall
down but Joe Lon and Willard wouldn't let him. The farmer
in the overalls slowly turned his back on them and sat staring down into his glass of whiskey.

Poncy was too weak to scream by the time the record
finally ended. He was soaked with sweat and his nostrils
were full of the thick smell of himself. They leaned inward
on him, hanging to his arms and clothing, their hot beery
breaths churning his stomach.

"Let's go to your place and eat snake," Willard finally
yelled at Joe Lon.

"He got snake?" said Duffy Deeter.

"He ain't got but about twenty," said Willard.

They'd turned Poncy loose and left him where he stood
in the middle of the dance floor, panting and sweating. It
was almost as if they had forgotten he was there now that they
had quit playing with him.

"I'll get us a little beer to ride on," said Duffy.

They were already heading for the door when Willard
stopped and went back to where Poncy was. He took him
by the shoulder and led him toward the door.

Joe Lon said: "Damn if I don't believe Enreeker's shit
on his sef."

"What?" said Hard Candy, crowding in to where he was.
"Where bouts?"

Poncy was walking stiff-legged with his thighs pressed
together. They got through the front door and out into the
weak afternoon sunlight.

Willard slapped Poncy on the back and said: "Hell, don't
feel bad. I shit on myself before."

"Me too," Joe Lon said, "lots of times."

Poncy turned his head uncertainly. "You have?"

"Sure, we . . ." said Willard. They had stopped in the
parking lot. Willard Miller's voice had trailed off and he held

the unfinished sentence like a measure. Then he said: "Sure, we all shit on ourselves, but *we* weren't but three months old."

Laughing and shouting they raced for the Winnebago and left Poncy standing in the parking lot gripping his thighs together in front of his little Porsche.

Susan Gender drove the Winnebago and Hard Candy sat on the seat beside her. Duffy and Willard and Joe Lon lay on the floor behind the seats. Willard and Duffy were singing. Joe Lon lay very still on his back and looked at the ceiling and thought about Poncy back there in the parking lot of the Blue Pines. He felt like he felt when he screamed at Elfie or hit her. He hadn't meant to hurt the old man, but he knew he had. He eased his hands down onto his flat hard stomach. Something in him was tearing loose. He felt it going more and more out of control. Duffy Deeter howled a song in his ear about a whore from Peoria. He wished to God he could escape. But he didn't know where he could go or what he wanted to escape from.

When they got to his purple double-wide, Joe Lon skinned snakes in a frenzy. He picked up the snakes by the tails as he dipped them out of the metal drums and swung them around and around his head and then popped them like a cowwhip, which caused their heads to explode. Then he nailed them up on a board in the pen and skinned them out with a pair of wire pliers. Elfie was standing in the door of the trailer behind them with a baby on her hip. Full of beer and fascinated with what Joe Lon was doing, none of them saw her. But Joe Lon could feel—or thought he could— the weight of her gaze on his back while he popped and skinned the snakes. He finally turned and looked at her, pulling his lips back from his teeth in a smile that only shamed him.

He called across the yard to her. "Thought we'd cook

up some snake and stuff, darlin, have ourselves a feast."

Her face brightened in the door and she said: "Course we can, Joe Lon, honey."

Elfie brought him a pan and Joe Lon cut the snakes into half-inch steaks. Duffy turned to Elfie and said: "My name's Duffy Deeter and this is something fine. Want to tell me how you cook up snakes?"

Elfie smiled, trying not to show her teeth. "It's lots a ways. Way I do mostly is I soak'm in vinegar about ten minutes, drain'm off good, and sprinkle me a little Looseanner redhot on'm, roll'm in flour, and fry'm is the way I mostly do."

"God," said Susan Gender.

Duffy Deeter slapped Joe Lon on the ass and said, "Where'd you get this little lady, boy? Damn if you haven't got you some little lady here."

Elfie blushed, and Joe Lon didn't answer. They followed him into the trailer. Joe Lon put on a stack of Merle Haggard and Elfie took the snake into the kitchen, where she wouldn't let the other two girls come, saying: "It ain't but room for one in a trailer kitchen. I'll cook it up in two shakes." Joe Lon got some beer out of the icebox and they all sat in the little living room looking out onto the campground. The babies lay in their playpen where their mother had put them, screaming and refusing to suck their sugartits. Joe Lon pulled at his beer and then said something to Hard Candy he'd been thinking on and off most of the afternoon.

"Why don't you call you house and tell that sister of yorn to come eat snake with us?" He was unable to make himself say the boy's name. "Tell'r to bring him that plays debate too if she feels like it. We got enough snake here for everbody."

Hard Candy got up and called her sister. Directly, she

came back and sat down. "Berenice said she'd be sliding in here in a sec but not to wait the snake on her."

They all sat now without talking, pulling easy on the beers, a little stunned with alcohol and exhausted with dancing. Susan Gender said she hoped they had not hurt the little Spic and that he'd get back to Mystic all right, but nobody wanted to talk about it, so they let it alone and watched the layering smoke over the campground above the open fires that were starting up now among the trailers and campers and tents. Although it was still about four hours until sundown, the afternoon was beginning to turn cool.

Joe Lon had just come back from the icebox with more beer when Berenice came sliding into the yard beside his pickup in her new Austin-Healy. She had two batons with her, and she came prancing through the door, turning her brilliant smile on all of them, and explaining that Shep had stayed to talk with her daddy because he was seriously considering becoming a brain surgeon.

"Besides," she said, a little breathless, beaming still, "the notion of a snake steak supper just made'm want to throw up. Shep's got delicate digestion." While she talked the batons slipped through her long slender hands in slow revolutions.

When neither Joe Lon nor Willard introduced them, Duffy said: "My name's Duffy Deeter. That's Miss Susan Gender. We're both from Gainesville." He gave her his own blinding smile. "Gainesville, Florida, not Georgia." Duffy was wondering if his head could withstand a serious scissors grip from those powerful baton-twirling thighs.

"Why that's the University of Florida, isn't it?" said Berenice, whose fine-grit voice education had turned to Cream of Wheat.

"I'm in philosophy and theater arts," said Susan. "Duffy's

not connected with the university. He's a lawyer."

"Oh, I do wish Shep had come. He's so interested in philosophy and theater arts and law. A mind like a sponge, just like a big old sponge." Susan and Duffy and Berenice beamed one upon the other. Joe Lon and Willard and Hard Candy sat bored and unsmiling and drunk along one wall.

Elfie came out of the kitchen wiping flour on her pretty apron. "We can eat any . . ." Elfie stopped and looked at Berenice. "Any time we want to we can eat," she said, a sad tentative smile fading on her mouth. "Hi, Berenice. I didn't know you was here."

Berenice high-stepped across the linoleum rug and hugged Elfie like a sister. "Just got here," she said. "Come through the door this minute. How you been, honey?" And without waiting for an answer: "You looking good. You looking one hundred percent." She turned and pointed to the two babies lying now curled in exhausted sleep in their playpen in the middle of the room. "You got two handsome little man-babies, honey. I was just looking and thinking how handsome them little darlings were."

Elfie blushed. "Thank you. Me and Joe Lon . . . Joe Lon and me, why, we think that . . . think that too."

"You want a drink?" said Joe Lon.

Berenice shifted her beatdown magnificent haunches and turned to look at him. "A little light something might be nice before we eat," she said.

"Oh, I'll get it," said Elfie quickly. "Let me get it."

"Let me help you," said Berenice.

"No, I can . . ." But the two of them were gone through the door together before she could finish.

When they were gone, Willard said: "She used to bubble a bottle like a goddam sawmill nigger. Now she wants a little light something. Jesus!"

"I got a little light something I'm gone give her," said Joe Lon.

"She needs to be opened up some so she can breathe," said Hard Candy, "that sister of mine does."

"You gone try to put wood to Berenice?" said Willard. "Right here in the trailer with the babies and the old lady standing around?"

"Shut up, Willard," said Joe Lon bitterly. "It ain't nothing funny."

"Don't tell me to shut up," said Willard Miller. "I'll come over there and let you smell you daddy's fist."

They sat glaring at each other, but Joe Lon was bored with the game. Seemed it was one game after another.

"I don't understand," said Duffy, but he already suspected he did. "Run it by me again."

"Them two used to be a case here in Lebeau County," said Willard evenly without ever taking his eyes off Joe Lon. "They used to be a case when Joe Lon here was Boss Snake of the Mystic Rattlers."

"She's a fine-looking girl," said Duffy Deeter.

"The world's full of fine-looking girls," Joe Lon said sourly.

"It ain't full of Berenices," said Willard. "Was, she couldn't strike a lick on you like she does."

"Then it must be my turn," said Joe Lon. "Git everybody out of the trailer after we eat them snakes."

"How the hell I'm sposed do that?" said Willard.

"You'll think of something," said Joe Lon. "You Boss Rattler now. It's you goddam job to think of something."

But he didn't think of something. He was not the one. It was Susan Gender at the suggestion of Duffy Deeter who thought of something. After they had eaten the snakes and after Lummy had brought another bottle of whiskey and stood around at the back door long enough to tell them how Big Joe had called the store for somebody to come and bury Old Tuffy, and Duffy Deeter had found out that tomorrow night there was going to be a dog fight—champion dogs on which money could be bet—after all of that, during which time Berenice had talked excitedly and in detail about her trip to Europe to study French and Joe Lon had sat listening, choking on both snake and the thought that he had spent *his* time and life selling nigger whiskey and watching Elfie's teeth fall out, they were once again cramped into the living room when Susan Gender said: "Hard Candy, let's go outside and have us a twirl-off. Settle this snake down some."

Susan Gender was excited. They were all excited, except Elfie, who sat feeding the babies Gerber's strained food out of little green and yellow bottles. They were excited because they watched Berenice still compulsively talking unaware that they were setting her up to be, as Hard Candy said, ventilated by Joe Lon, who by this time had his game face on and was ready to work.

"We can settle the snake and you can all be judges," said Susan Gender. "You feel up to a twirl-off, Hard Candy?"

"Always," said Hard Candy.

"You're up against a good one," said Berenice. "My sister is a good one." She crossed her strong baton-twirling thighs and Duffy Deeter thought Joe Lon would fall out of his chair. They were only waiting for Elfie to finish spooning the last jar of Gerber's into the older baby. "We both went, you know, to the Dixie National Baton Twirling Institute for two summers. Two summers each, both of us."

"Jesus," Duffy said. "Really?" Besides liking the marvelously absurd ring of *Dixie National Baton Twirling Institute*, he loved the excited enthusiastic way Berenice had been babbling ever since she got there.

"Right," she said. "It's on the campus of Old Miss."

"Dynamite," said Duffy.

She talked on, a little breathlessly, waving her hands, her eyes turning now and again to check Elfie's progress with the baby food.

"When we were there the Director of the Institute was Don Sartell. He's known as Mister Baton, you know."

"I didn't know that," said Duffy. He was wishing he and Joe Lon could double-team her little ass and thereby force her to give up all her secrets.

"I'm done," said Elfie, turning her ruined smile on them. "This youngan ain't eatin another bite."

"Let's get to that twirl-off," said Duffy. He looked at Elfie. "Want to take the playpen outside for the babies?"

"Oh, they'll sleep now they full," she said. "We can leave'm right where they are."

They let Elfie pass first through the door followed by Willard, Susan Gender, Hard Candy, and finally Duffy, who cast one lingering look over his shoulder toward Berenice just passing in front of Joe Lon. Joe Lon's face was gray and tight. He looked a little out of control. Duffy closed the door.

As the door closed Joe Lon took her arm and spun her to face him. "Don't!" Berenice said. "God, we can't, not here."

"Oh, I magine we can," he said.

She wasn't listening. She'd already broken one of her nails tearing at his belt. He took her by the wrist and led her down the short narrow hallway to a little room and threw her on the bed.

"Git naked and take a four-point stance," he said.

The bed was right next to a wall and she braced herself firmly against the window ledge. He struck her from behind like she'd been a tackling dummy.

"You'll make me holler," Berenice said.

"Holler then," said Joe Lon Mackey.

"You know how I always holler," she said quickly. And then: "Oh, Jesus, honey, honey, honey Jesus."

"Is that what you gone holler?" he demanded. "Is it *Jesus honey*?"

She could no longer talk. He had driven her close against the window. The blinds were drawn, but around the edge, through a half inch of warped glass, he could see Hard Candy and Susan where they were twirling off while Willard and Duffy and Elfie squatted on the hard-packed dirt, watching. Elfie kept turning back to stare at the trailer, sometimes right at the window where they were locked together looking out. Berenice's hair lay in a damp tangle on her neck. Sweat ran on their bodies, darkening the sheet under them.

Joe Lon held the sharp blades of her hip bones, one in each hand, while he looked absently through the window. Berenice slowly turned her head to gaze fondly back at him over her shoulder.

"I must tell you, darling," she said, "I love Shep."

He told himself that he didn't care one way or the other if she loved Shep but that talk of love was the last thing in the world he wanted to hear from her. From anybody. He refused to meet her eyes and finally she turned to gaze with him through the warped glass at Elfie where she still squatted outside the trailer with Willard Miller and Duffy Deeter.

"It doesn't mean I didn't love you," she said.

"I don't want to hear about it," he said. "I don't need that."

"All right," she said.

Outside, Elf turned to look quickly back toward the trailer but then she didn't look any more because Willard put his hand on her shoulder and started talking to her, pointing at the girls, who were taking turns testing each other in complicated little dance routines, their silver batons flashing like swords in the sun. In the other room the babies slowly started crying, almost like singing, a chorus of something sad and interminable.

In a light conversational voice while they watched Susan Gender skip across the bare dirt yard outside, Berenice said: "You know, darling, baton twirling is the second biggest young girls' movement in America. Did you know that? Uh huh, is though. Girl Scouts is Numero Uno. That means first. But baton twirling is *the* biggest if you don't count Girl Scouts." She turned to smile at him over her shoulder. "The reason is . . . well, there's three of them." She didn't look back at him, but she braced herself with one hand and held up the other hand with three fingers for him to see. "Three. First you don't have to go nowheres. You can do it in the living room or like them out in the yard—out in the yard. Second. No expensive equipment. Third. You can practice alone."

"What good is it?" said Joe Lon.

"What?"

"I said what good is it?"

"Here, think about this. Did you know there's a *Who's Who in Baton Twirling*?"

Joe Lon said, "Studying them goddam foreign languages is done ruint you mind."

"You honey," she said, smiling back at him as she did. He made her grunt. She had to use two hands to keep from being punched through the window.

He watched Elfie glancing over her shoulder toward the trailer, ignoring the splits, the whirls, the twirling flashing batons. He did not know what love was. And he did not know what good it was. But he knew he carried it around with him, a scabrous spot of rot, of contagion, for which there was no cure. Rage would not cure it. Indulgence made it worse, inflamed it, made it grow like a cancer. And it had ruined his life. Not now, not in this moment. Long before. The world had seemed a good and livable place. Brutal, yes, but there was a certain joy in that. The brutality on the football field, in the tonks, was celebration. Men were maimed without malice, sometimes—often even—in friendship. Lonely, yes. Running was lonely. Sweat was lonely. The pain of preparation was lonely. There's no way to share a pulled hamstring with somebody else. There's no way to farm out part of a twisted knee. But who in God's name ever assumed otherwise? Once you knew that it was all bearable.

But love, love seemed to mess up everything. It *had* messed up everything. He could not have said it, but he knew it. It was knowledge that he carried in his blood. Elfie was watching the window through which he was looking. He felt her eyes on his eyes. And the wavering window glass made her face softer, more vulnerable and afflicted with the pain of child-bearing than he could stand to look at.

The golden plain of Berenice's back, gently indented along the spine by twin rolls of smooth muscle, was speckled with glittering drops of sweat. The musking odor of her came to his flared nostrils like something steaming off a stove. She was still talking, had never stopped talking.

". . . see, it's beginning solo, intermediate solo, advanced solo, strutting—beginning and military (I was always good at strutting)—two baton, fire baton, duet, trio and team . . ."

It was a wonder Big Joe had not killed his mother. Everybody thought it a miracle that he had not. In many ways, Joe Lon knew, it would have been better if he had. If Big Joe had simply and quickly blown her head off with a shotgun his little sister might not today be lying in a bed stinking of her own shit.

The babies were screaming louder now. The older boy

was banging the barred side of his playpen in a rage with his rattle. Out in the yard Elfie sat with her eyes steadily on the room where he held Berenice, she still compulsively talking, in her four-point stance. Susan Gender and Hard Candy Sweet were no longer twirling. They seemed to be in an argument about something, their fists balled on their hips, their legs straddling.

". . . and they arguing right now because competition is exact. It's exact, Joe Lon, in your twirl-off, it is. In each one it's a judge and a scorekeeper. The scorekeeper . . ."

His mother had left for reasons of love. Deserted them all: Big Joe, himself, his sister Beeder, the big house. And in deserting them had left an enormous ragged hole in their lives.

The note had said. *I have gone with Billy. Forgive me. But I love him and I have gone with him.*

They knew who Billy was well enough. He was a traveling shoe salesman, and Mystic was one of his stops. It had been for years. He was short and nearly bald, a soft, almost feminine-looking man who always wore the same shiny wrinkled suit and drove a rusting Corvair car. And the bitterest, most painful thing Joe Lon ever had to do was admit to himself that his mother had been fucking that little shoe salesman for reasons of love when she had a house and a husband and children and a flower garden and friends and a hometown and a son famous through the whole South and meals to cook and clothes to wash, a woman like that—no, not a woman, his *mother*—lying down on her back with a little man who walked always leaning slightly to the right from carrying a heavy suitcase full of shoe samples.

". . . oh, it's exact all right, the competition is. You take your advanced solo, for instance." She moved her hips languidly against him as she talked. "Your advance solo has to last at least two minutes and twenty seconds and not more than two minutes and thirty seconds."

Big Joe had gone and gotten her. Billy lived in Atlanta and Big Joe had gone there and found his wife sitting in a little ratty flat on the edge of a neighborhood full of niggers (Big Joe had given all the details day in and day out for a year after it happened), found his wife sitting alone because Billy was out on his sales route with his suitcase full of shoes and Big Joe had picked her up and brought her home. It was morning when they got back to Mystic and Joe Lon and Beeder were in school. Beeder came home that afternoon still wearing her little tassled uniform from her cheerleading practice and found her mother sitting in her favorite rocker wearing Big Joe's tie. She was wearing her husband's tie and had a one-sentence note pinned to her cotton dress. Beeder had never been the same since.

". . . and Ole Miss, the home of the Dixie National Baton Twirling Institute, is in Oxford, Mississippi, the home of William Faulkner."

His daddy didn't own but one suit of clothes, a black thing made out of heavy wool cloth, which he almost never wore except to certain championship dog fights. The cuffs and sleeves were spotted with old blood. And since he didn't own but one suit he didn't find it necessary to own but one tie, which was black too. He never untied it but simply loosened it until it would slide over his head and then hung it in the closet like a noose. When Beeder opened the door she had found her mother sitting in the rocker with a plastic bag over her head and the tie cinched tightly at her throat. Her starting eyes were open under the plastic and her face was blue. The note pinned over her breast was not addressed to anyone. It said: *bring me back now you son of a bitch.*

Through the window it looked as though Susan Gender

and Hard Candy would fight. Both Duffy and Willard were on their feet now and between them but it looked as though they would start swinging their batons any minute. It was an old movie and he had seen it too many times to find it anything but boring. It no longer entertained. He pulled Berenice away from the window and turned her over. She moved to his easiest touch, smiling fondly upon him, but insisting upon talking of love.

". . . first met Shep I knew I'd marry him but I'd always love . . . love . . ."

"Take it," he said softly.

He held her by her perfectly formed pink ears and guided his cock into her mouth, which she took willingly and deeply, her eyes still turned up, watching him where he was propped on Elf's pillow. She sucked like a calf at its mother and he never released her ears, forcing himself so deep she could only make little humming noises.

Finally he said: "I want you ass."

She withdrew her throat and mouth and said as she turned, "You honey you honey you can have my . . . easy darling be *easy*." But he wasn't easy at all because he knew she was about to talk of love and he had her bowed almost double, plunging deeply into her ass by the time she got to the place where she could say, "But I can love you too, love you with all my heart, love . . ."

"Love," said Joe Lon, "is taking it out of you mouth and sticking in you ass."

"Yes," she said, "oh, yes, that's . . ."

"But *true* love," he said, "goddam *true* love is taking it out of you ass and sticking it in you mouth." He flipped her like a doll and she—flushed and swooning—went down in a great spasm of joy, sucking like a baby before she ever got there.

Lottie Mae had been told to go back to Big Joe's to cook again, but Brother Boy had not been sent with her this time and she did not go. She had meant to go, or rather she meant to do what her mother told her to do but she quickly forgot what that was or where she was going so she had been wandering about the streets of Mystic for more than an hour.

She carefully listened to the talk of snakes, knowing that if she listened closely enough she would find out what the snake had in mind for her and maybe avoid it. She walked and listened and watched terrified. The world had become dangerous. What she had always feared would happen had happened, although she did not know it was what she feared until it happened.

White people were dangerous and snakes were dangerous and now the two were working together, each doing what the other told it to. She was sure she had seen a snake in a weeded ditch with the head of a white man. Right after she came out of the house on the way to Big Joe's, which she had immediately forgotten, she saw it, long and black and diamond-patterned in the ditch with a white man's head. It had blue eyes. The bluest eyes any white man ever had. She was sure she had seen it. She thought she had seen it. Maybe it was only a dream or a memory of another time. Whatever it was, she still saw it every time she closed her eyes, coiled there on the back of her eyelids, blue-eyed and dangerous.

She went over to the school ground and was not surprised to find the idol they had made. She knew it was not a real snake, that it was made out of paper and glue to be bigger than any snake could ever be, but she also knew why they had made it, and the only thing that surprised her was that no one knelt there in worship. Instead of worship there was much laughter and drinking and eating and dancing about in an unseemly way. They were white people though and there was nothing they could have done that would have surprised her.

She kept careful watch for the snake with the man's head and the clear blazing blue eyes. She watched the ditches and the weeds and even the limbs of trees. You never knew that it was not hanging there overhead waiting for you to come walking by. If it had blue eyes, might it not have anything, any ability or talent or evil design?

Lottie Mae watched and waited. She knew very well what was coming. There was nothing she could do about it. She was resigned to the risk, to the consequences, to the world and what it had brought her. Which didn't mean she was not afraid. She walked about with an icy panic flooding her heart. But at last knowing there was no alternative, there was a kind of benumbed calmness rooted in her bones.

"Hey, girl, you want this?"

Lottie Mae turned slowly to the man who had spoken to her. He was white, deeply sun-burned with a black stubble of beard. His overalls were stuffed into high boots and around his neck was a snake, thin as a whip and clay-colored. The snake held its cat-eyed head aloft, its tongue waving and darting on the air. The man drew the snake from around his neck, and it immediately wrapped itself about his forearm. The slick and shining head lay in the palm of his hand like a plum. The man was smiling as he edged closer to where she stood.

"Ain't nothing but a lil ole snake," he said. "You ain't scared of no snake are you, girl?"

Lottie Mae did not move. She stood ready. The snake, it seemed to her, knew she was ready. It lay in the open palm without lifting its head.

"You do wrong for a quarter, girl?" said the man.

She turned and started home. The man did not follow her but stood calling to her to come back and see his snake. She walked past the platform where the Rattlesnake Queen would be crowned. It had been covered in bright red cloth. It was very pretty. She wished, if things did not have to be the way they were, that she could have some cloth like that. It would make a pretty dress. Or maybe a shirt for Brother Boy. But there was no use thinking about that. The snake had seen her. She had seen the snake. She was as ready as she could make herself. There was no use in thinking about making dresses and shirts. And there was no use in hiding.

A man was sitting on the side of a ditch. She first saw him because she was keeping her eye on the ditches, watching for the snake. But she kept watching him because his hair reminded her of snakes, might have been snakes, the tufts of white hair rose in such wild twists. He was an old man, and as she got closer, she heard him talking, almost chanting. She did not take her eyes off him.

"Snakes, not sons, wreathing around the bones of Tiriel!" he cried, "God hath said ye shall not eat of it, neither shall ye touch it, lest ye die. And the serpent said unto the woman, ye shall not surely die!"

She went on by, drawing her mother's cotton neck-wrapper closer under her chin. There was a little bit of a bite in the air now that it was getting on toward dark. She could no longer remember why she was walking out here among all these white people anyway. There was not another black man or woman anywhere and she could not imagine why she had decided to come out here and deliberately walk where none of her people—not her mother or her father or any of her uncles—ever came in these yearly roundups of snakes. Maybe it was only by showing herself, she thought, to the danger of the snake that she could show that she was not afraid of the snake. She knew, she had been told by her uncles, that snakes were cowards. They ran. They hid. They took advantage. The rattle was only a desperate effort not to be stepped upon, a frantic effort not to have to face anything that might want to fight, that might have a chance in a fight.

She was almost to the little road that led back through a pine thicket toward her mother's house when she saw the blue light pulsing around her, lighting the trunks of trees and the dead brown grass on the sides of the little road. She didn't even look back. She stopped and stood without moving. Even when she heard the engine of the car and the light got close enough so that she could feel it on the skin of her face she did not look. She knew before she heard his voice. And somehow she knew he had brought the snake she had been waiting for, or maybe the snake had brought him. It did not matter. She would have to deal with the snake. She was the one.

"Git in here, Lot, goddammit, I been looking everwhere for you," said Buddy Matlow.

The door swung open and there he was on the far side, leaning toward her, gazing up at her from beneath the flat brim of his sheriff's hat.

She stood looking at him.

"Git in here, I ain't got all day!"

She got in.

"Well, close the door, you sweet thing."

She closed the door and Buddy Matlow found a little open space in the wall of pine bordering the road and spun his Plymouth in a circle and roared back down the road. Lottie Mae waited, tense but still with the numb calmness running in her, preparing herself for what she knew she had to do.

"How you been, Lottie Mae?"

"I been all right, Mistuh Buddy."

"Goddammit, Lottie Mae, how many times I got to tell you don't call me Mister? How many times, huh?"

"Yessuh," she said.

"That too, dammit." He reached across and touched her hands where they lay stiff in her lap. "Don't call me Mister. Don't ever do that again."

"All right," she said.

"Ain't I already told you I loved you?"

"Yessuh," she said.

"Jesus," he said, one-handing the Plymouth through a tight turn on a dirt road about a mile south of Mystic. "You do it again I'm gone have to slap the shit out of you. Now that's the simple truth, Lottie Mae. One thing I cain't stand it's somebody I told I loved'm to keep on calling me Mister and like that." He stopped talking, caught in a fit of coughing. "It ain't seemly."

"I won't do it no more. Less I forgit. It be hard not to forgit."

"You tell anybody about the snake?" he said.

"What it was?" she said quickly.

He sighed and rolled his eyes up toward the brim of his hat. "Lottie Mae, try not to talk nigger talk to me."

"What snake it was?"

"Don't be scared," he said. "I ain't talking about a snake, anyhow. I'm talking about me. About at the jail. You tell anybody about that?"

"Ain't say nothing."

"Good," he said. "Be kind of stupid anyway wouldn't it? Honey, you got fucked last night by a United States of America Veet Nam hero and former captain of the Ramlin Wrecks from Georgia Tech. Here, you want a drink of this?" He held out a bottle of whiskey toward her.

"Make me sick," she said.

"This ain't gone make you sick. It's from Mr. Joe Lon's place a bidness. Hell, it was George sold it to me. Go on and take youself a drink."

"I hafta?" she said, not looking at him.

"You have to," he said.

She didn't really mind taking a drink of the whiskey. Unless it made her sick. She didn't want to be sick when she had to face the snake. Her fight wasn't with Mr. Buddy Matlow. Her fight was with the snake. She took the bottle out of his hand. It burned her throat a little but then settled in her stomach, warming it like one of her mother's meal poultices. It was the first brown whiskey she had ever had, although she'd seen it. The few times she'd ever tasted white whiskey it had made her immediately sick. This brown whiskey was better.

"These goddam snakes already about run me crazy," said Buddy Matlow, "and we still got tomorrow to go."

"Snakes be bad," she said.

"Damn truth," he said. "Ever year, I say, no more snakes, and ever year I git right in the middle of it." He glanced at her. "How that drink doing you?"

"Be doin fine," she said.

"Good," he said. Then: "Well, somebody got to keep these goddam fools from killing each other. Weren't for me, these sumbitches would eat each other alive. It's been times when they damn nigh done it spite of me."

"I don't misdoubt it," she said.

"Want another drink?"

"No."

He took a long pull at the bottle and then leaned across and flipped down the glove compartment and put the bottle in it. He fumbled there for a moment, and then flipped the door shut.

"I was looking for you this morning," he said. "Where the hell you been?"

She told him about her mother having the miseries, about how she had to go cook for Mr. Big Joe and Beeder.

"Shit," he said, "I was over there myself to see that dog of his'n. Musta just missed you over there. I'm gone put ever goddam thing I got in hock to go on his dog Tuff." He laughed. "Might even mortgage this fuckin Plymouth car." Then seriously: "Did you see that girl of his, Beeder?"

"Uh huh," said Lottie Mae. She wondered why he kept squirming around over there in his seat. He was worse than Little Brother in church. But she didn't look. She didn't want to know. She stared straight ahead into the gathering darkness.

"You feeling good?" he said.

She still did not look at him. She spoke to the dark flashing trees beyond the headlights. "Where you taking me?"

"It's all right," he said.

"Where you taking me?"

"I ain't seen Beeder Mackey in . . . what is it now? I was three years ahead of Joe Lon at Mystic High—none of the colored went there then—and he was two years ahead of Willard. Shit, I ain't seen that girl in, it must be six years. What does she look like now, anyway?"

"Watch that TeeVee of hern," she said. "An stay in her room."

"Seem like to me she was gone grow into sompin real good," he said. "That's what I remember."

They drove down a dirt road in silence. Finally he said: "But you feeling all right now, right? You feeling all right?" When she didn't answer, he said, "All right. That's fine with me. I don't want to talk either. Look here what I got. Look at it. Right here. See."

She knew without looking that this was what he had

looked for her for and what he had brought her in the sheriff's car for and that there was nothing else she could do but look. She turned her head and saw a snake standing in his lap. Right in his lap a snake rose straight as a plumb line, no striking coil in its body but arrow straight on its tail, and at the top of its body the mouth was stretched and she could see the needle fangs like tiny swords. It was the snake she had been waiting for, that she had been preparing for since that morning in Beeder's room.

"How about that?" he said. "What do you think?"

She did not answer but in a movement she had been practicing in her mind all day she bent to her ankle where the straight razor was wedged inside her shoe and in a single fluid movement she struck his lap and came away with the snake in her hand, its softening head with the needle fangs still showing just above her thumb and forefinger.

She raised it aloft and was amazed that it did not struggle but hung limp from her hand utterly dead and beaten. She raised her eyes to Buddy Matlow's and found him staring over the wheel of the Plymouth, his face leached of all color, his lips struggling to speak and pointing to his lap where now a fountain of blood shot into the air and ran over his legs and dripped down into the floorboard of the car.

"You . . . you . . . cut it off." He finally managed to say.

She said: "I always known I could. I always known I would."

She opened the door and got out. Buddy Matlow struggled behind the wheel. He looked at her and made a noise, not a word, just a noise. There was still no pain, but he had gone instantly light-headed with terror and loss of blood. He knew he was dying. He knew he ought to be doing something, but he did not know what it was. Lottie Mae bent and looked at him through the window.

"Wait," said Buddy Matlow. "Wait."

"Be through now," she said and walked away from the car. She did not walk slow, but she did not walk fast either. She had done what she had waited all day to do. She remembered where she was going, that her mother had sent her to Big Joe's, that she was supposed to help Miss Beeder.

She had to walk past the school and the open field where they did the football. There were more people there and more noise and more open fires than she had ever dreamed there could be in one place at one time in the whole world. In the middle of all the people was a snake, three stories tall standing against the darkening sky, coiled to strike. She kept to the edge of the crowd in the gathering dusk and was not afraid.

At Big Joe's, she went directly to Beeder's room and Beeder asked immediately: "Did they burn the snake yet?"

"What it was. You gone have to talk it up?"

Beeder watched Lottie Mae's slow purple mouth move in the flickering light. But Lottie Mae was already turning to watch the television. Her eyes and teeth were now brilliant in her face. She licked her lips and squinted and did not answer. Tanks roared across the land. Airplanes dropped bombs. Geysers of sand and stone and bits of metal flew from the earth. A turbaned woman knelt beside a man and rocked and wept. She finally turned her face up toward the black sky where airplanes still dropped bombs. She screamed and looked as though she had no lips, as though the lips had been cut away from her dry broken teeth.

Lottie Mae recognized the man who talked when the guns and the planes and the bombs stopped. It was the NBC Nightly News. It was Lottie Mae's favorite program. Much better than the detective stories where you had to put up with a lot of talking and fooling around before you got to the good parts. NBC Nightly News went straight to the robbing and killing, the crying and the blood, burning buildings and mashed cars. Them NBC Nightly News sumbitches was mean. Soon kill you as look at you. Killed somebody ever night. Sometimes drowned whole towns in the ocean. Or made babies grow together at the shoulder.

A man had come on now trying to sell Ford automobiles: "The closer you look, the better we look!"

Beeder and Lottie Mae's eyes left the screen at the same time and their gaze joined across the soiled bed.

"I didn't hear you," shouted Beeder. "They burn the snake or not?" Then when Lottie Mae still did not answer: "Anybody hurt?"

"Not I'm a mind of."

"Didn't fall on anybody, nobody burned, no bones broke?"

"I ain't seen it."

They were shouting at each other. It was the only way they could be heard over the NBC Nightly News.

"Can we turn hit down?"

"What?"

"Turn hit *down*, the TeeVee!"

"What?" shouted Beeder.

Lottie Mae went over and turned the television all the way down. Beeder sat up in bed. "What did you do that for?"

"I wanted to tell you. I cut hit off."

"You ain't got no call to turn my TeeVee down. Now turn it back up."

"I cut hit off at the ground. Shrunk hit up till hit wont no biggern you little finger."

Beeder was beside herself. "This room's mine! What I say goes."

"Tetched it one time with this and hit come off in my hand just like a natural thing."

Lottie Mae was holding a straight razor up in front of

her. The blade was honed thin and bright and terrible. Beeder stopped shouting. She got quietly off the bed and adjusted the sound so she could hear it but not so loud they had to shout. She stood beside Beeder and they both watched the thin shiny steel razor for a long time.

"Tell me," said Beeder glancing apprehensively at the far wall.

"See," said Lottie Mae with enormous satisfaction. "Hit were this snake."

"Yes," said Beeder.

"Hit tetched me all the living while. Went to sleep with me, snake did. Woke up with me. Eat my food. Come in the front door with me, went out the back. Wore my skin like clothes."

"Wore your skin like clothes," Beeder said.

"Close as breathing," said Lottie Mae. "Looked into my eyes. Breathed into my nose. Put his taste on my tongue—all up in my mouth—and made me swaller him. Felt him grow in my hair, move in my stomach. When I went on my knees to pray, snake had the ear of the lord."

"You was scared?" Beeder asked.

"Scared to death," said Lottie Mae.

"You cry?"

"All the time."

"And was you afraid to go out?"

"Wouldn't *go out* less I had to."

"And was you afraid to come in?"

"Wouldn't come *in neither* less I had to."

"It had you covered all around," said Beeder.

"All around. In the air and on my plate. Everthing that moved say snake. Snake! It was you say what I might do. It's why I come back to tell you. You was right. Just hit that snake with a razor. Tetch hit. One time. Gone forever.

Outta my air. Outta my plate. Don't tetch my skin like clothes."

"All because of the razor."

"That snake shrunk up and died like magic."

"Listen," said Beeder. "Hear it?"

"I *tol* you less turn it down."

"Not the TeeVee. *That!*"

Lottie Mae folded her razor and put it in her shoe. "Cain't hear nothin but the TeeVee."

"Here then," said Beeder. She reached over and turned the sound all the way off, and rising out of the silence it left —coming from behind the far wall—was a ragged thumping like the beating of an enormous erratic heart.

"Hear it now?"

Lottie Mae cocked her head and regarded the wall. "I do hear."

"He's got another one tied in there."

"I don't misdoubt it," Lottie Mae said. "Be one tied everwhere you look these days."

"He'll tie another one on it before he's through," said Beeder.

They stood for a long time watching the place beyond the wall where the thing was thumping.

Finally Lottie Mae said: *"Before he's through, he gone tie everone on it."*

"Well," said Shep Martin, "I thought law."

Dr. Sweet drew on his pipe and slowly wagged his huge white head. His skin and eyes and hair and even the suit he was wearing was the color of damp chalk. He looked as though he had not been in the sun for a year, which was true, since he actively cultivated a bleached look. He thought it made him look scholarly.

"I myself," said Dr. Sweet, "once seriously thought of the law." He enjoyed these young men his daughters brought home, all of them on the edge of beginning to live their lives, all of them so full of hope and the higher virtues. "But, alas, it was to be medicine that I finally chose. I've not regretted it either."

They were sitting in Dr. Sweet's living room in front of a large fire, roaring in a fieldstone fireplace. Mrs. Sweet was upstairs asleep and the doctor had let his black maid go for the evening.

"It must be very rewarding," said Shep.

"A doctor is able to do much very decent work out here in the . . ." He chuckled deeply in his good gray throat. ". . . in the provinces, so to speak."

"You ought to think of writing, Doctor Sweet," said Shep. "You certainly can . . ." Here he gave his own radio announcer's chuckle. "Certainly can *turn a phrase*."

The doctor waved his hand. "When I retire I plan to devote my life to *belles lettres*." He smiled. "But for now, I have to keep this county as healthy and wholesome as modern medicine will allow."

"There must be great satisfaction in that," said Shep.

"No more than you'll find in the practice of law, young man. Law is an admirable calling."

"I haven't actually decided," said Shep. "But you see, sir, I'm on the debate team and doing extremely . . ."

The doorbell, a three-chimed gong, floated through the house. The doctor raised his eyes to the ceiling and wagged his head. "Probably not a patient," he said, "but it would not surprise me if it was. Nobody thinks a doctor sleeps or needs time for reflection." He sighed and got to his feet.

"Perhaps a crisis," said Shep.

The doctor, walking toward the door, said: "You soon find in medicine that to a patient everything is a crisis. Everything from a rash to a . . . ."

He did not finish but opened the door and found Buddy Matlow, pale, his mouth like a razor-cut in his face, looking down upon him. "Well, Sheriff," said the doctor, looking past Buddy toward the night sky because he had not heard the rain start and certainly it had not looked like rain and yet here was the sheriff standing in his raincoat, a yellow rubber slicker that fell well below his knees so that you could see only the point of one cowboy boot and about two and a half inches of a peg leg. It did not seem to be raining. "Come in. Come in."

Buddy Matlow's thin mouth stretched as though he would speak but he did not. It was almost a kind of yawn and then the lips came weakly back together. The doctor thought maybe Buddy was coming down with a cold. Colds seemed to do these big fellows worse than it did ordinary folk. Buddy had been leaning, holding to the door jamb with one of his wide square hands. Now he turned loose and leaned in toward the living room. His eyes wandered slowly from Dr. Sweet to the fireplace to the boy whom he had not met.

Shep stood up and came toward him with his hand out. Buddy Matlow came over the door sill, his wooden leg thumping on the floor. It was the thumping of the wooden leg that made Shep look down and see that the peg leg was leaving a wide round puddle of blood every time it stopped. Shep stood amazed with his hand out. When he raised his eyes he saw that the sheriff was holding what looked like a toy snake tenderly between the thumb and forefinger of his right hand. With his other hand, the sheriff was fumbling with the snaps on the yellow raincoat.

"Wait!" cried Shep. "Wait a minute!" He knew the man was about to show him what was under the coat and he knew he did not want to see it.

They saw the blood before the coat was all the way open. Buddy was slick with blood. The doctor did not move. From Buddy's shoulders to his knees he was smooth and slick with creamy gouts of blood. And it was obvious that it was coming from between his legs. Doctor Sweet was numb. His mind had simply quit. The worst he had ever seen was a man whose tongue had been deliberately split in two by a knife, and another man who had been scalped. But they had both been dead when he saw them. And they had both been black. But this. He knew from the blood, from the *nature* of the bleeding, what had happened and so he could not make himself move from where he stood as Buddy slowly reached out and put the toy snake in Shep's outstretched hand. Shep accepted the snake because he was unable to do anything else. It was bloody on the end and tiny and as he watched unbelieving the whole inside of the snake slipped out into his palm and it was a dick.

In a little voice that was cracked and whining, Shep said: "Somebody's cut his dick off." He turned to the doctor for his statement to be denied but the doctor was already sliding to the floor in a faint.

They could not get her father on the phone, and of course it was not her father they wanted, but Shep. Berenice, red-faced, her cheeks brittle with exhaustion, had insisted that she would not go if Shep could not be raised on the phone and brought to her side to go with her. They were all standing in Joe Lon's living room waiting to go see the thirty-foot snake burned and find out who was going to be crowned Miss Rattlesnake of the 1975 Roundup.

Duffy Deeter said: "Gender here's got more goddam

trophies'n I have." He waved vaguely at her. "Beauty," he said. Since he had gotten good and drunk, Duffy had called Susan by her last name.

"I was in one or two contests back in Alabama," said Susan.

"Shit, we had Miss Rattlesnake in the family two years back to back," said Hard Candy.

"I won my senior year," said Berenice. Now that the talk had turned to contests, she didn't seem quite as tired as before.

"I took it my sophomore," Hard Candy said.

"I . . . I . . ." They all turned to see Elfie in the door coming from the hallway. "I best git them babies ready for the sitter." She had forgotten not to smile—and it wasn't a smile anyway, a deep painful-looking grin rather—but she remembered as soon as they turned to her that she was showing her bad teeth and so she clamped shut her lips as deliberately as she might close a door. Joe Lon saw it all, saw how hurt and intimidated she was, and could have killed her, or killed them for making him want to kill her.

"I think we ought to stand here and see if we cain't talk it to death," said Willard Miller.

"Gender can talk anything to death," Duffy Deeter said, directing his thousand-yard stare at the near wall.

A girl of about eleven with hair the color of corn and a running nose had come to stay with the babies. She sat quietly in the corner, sucking at her nose.

"For Christ's sake let's get out of here," said Joe Lon, "before they burn the snake without us."

"I'll goddam drink to that," said Susan Gender. They'd called the twirl-off a draw and she wasn't happy with it. Both she and Hard Candy had promptly forgotten they had gone out there to start with to get Elfie out of the house. As soon as they got to twirling they forgot all about Joe Lon ventilating Hard Candy's sister and would have gotten into a fight with the batons if Duffy and Willard had not separated them, which Duffy had to convince Willard to help him do because Willard wanted to see them fight.

They all followed Joe Lon out into the yard, where it was already dark enough so they could see the light of an enormous fire on the school ground.

"Shit," said Willard, "they already burning the snake."

"That's a bonfire," said Hard Candy. "That's not the snake."

Saying she had to find Shep before she did anything else, Berenice got in her car and roared out of the yard, the rear end fishtailing and sending clay and gravel back in a steady arching line.

"What the hell ails her?" said Willard.

"She do seem a little edgy, don't she," said Hard Candy.

"She oughta calm down now some," said Joe Lon.

"I magine," said Susan Gender.

Elfie took Joe Lon's arm. "Let's go, honey."

She and Joe Lon got in the pickup. Willard left Hard Candy's car in the yard and drove over with Duffy and Susan Gender in the Winnebago. The Winnebago followed the pickup and they went slow because cars and campers and trucks were parked everywhere, on the sides of the road, in the ditches, and people—many of them children lost off from their parents—wandered in and among the parked vehicles.

"I wisht you wouldn't treat me like a fool, Joe Lon, honey," said Elfie.

"What?" said Joe Lon, narrowly missing a man carrying a snake.

"I ain't a fool," she said. "It's some might think I am, but I ain't a fool. You oughten to treat me like I was. Particular in front of strangers."

"I never said you was a fool."

"You sometimes got to act like I am."

"I do the best I can. I cain't do but one thing at the time."

"I know that."

"You don't know nothing."

"I might know more'n you think I know."

"This don't get us nowheres," said Joe Lon. "I don't want nothing nasty with you."

"What?"

"I don't want to be nasty," he said.

"All right, Joe Lon, honey."

They had to walk the last quarter mile because the road was choked full of parked cars and campers and pickups parked in every possible attitude, on the shoulder of the road and even in the ditches. They moved slowly, sometimes having to climb on bumpers and over hoods, Duffy Deeter cursing more or less steadily and threatening to make Susan carry him.

"Goddammit, Gender, you liable to have to care me the rest of the way."

"I'd known it was gone be like this," said Elfie, "I'd stayed with the youngans, what I'd done."

They finally stopped in the dark shadow of the oak trees. There was a band up on the stage where the Queen would be crowned. A wide piece of cloth tilted through the space over their heads saying they were called SLICK, SLIMEY, AND THE SNAKES. Slick and Slimey were the stage names of twin boys who lived four miles out of town on a peanut farm. They both played guitar and all of the members of the Snakes were also members of the Mystic Rattlers Marching High School Band. They wore skin-tight jumpsuits with little sequins sewn into them.

Men and women were packed in under the oak trees and around the stage. As far as Joe Lon could see, heads—close together and seemingly solid as the ground—bobbed and pulsed in an undulating wave to the rhythm of the music. On the little rise of ground where the papier mâché snake was built, a circling line of dancers had formed.

"It ain't no room to do nothing," said Elfie. "What we gone do with all these people?"

Duffy Deeter had already said something in the way of answering that, but only a word or two when a deep guttural sound came out of the shadows behind them and an enormous form moved solidly out of the darkness and stopped in a three-point stance shouting: *"dowwwn!"* Both Willard and Joe Lon spun and dropped in a crouch. *"Seeetttt!"* They took a three-point stance, head up, back flat, the rear foot digging in. "On twwwoooo!" Then: "Hut *one*! Hut *two*!" And they both fired out and were caught, one on each shoulder, and straightened up. The man who caught them was growling and slobbering and they were growling and slobbering and Duffy and the rest of them jumped out of the way because they thought Joe Lon and Willard were about to be driven back but they dug in after they had been straightened up and fought off the man by giving him several shots to the short ribs with their elbows and a few butts with their heads so that finally they had him all the way back and falling, with them on top. They rolled about in the dirt under the oak tree, growling no longer but all three of them laughing.

"You boys git up!" said the snarling voice in the dark of the oak tree where they were rolling around. "By damn, two on one and me a old man!"

Willard and Joe Lon came out of the shadows followed by the man who had caught them as they fired out of their three-point stance and straightened them up. He was a half inch taller than either of the boys and maybe sixty pounds heavier, with a great swinging gut under his shirt. He walked bowlegged and slightly pigeon-toed, rolling on the balls of his feet. His face was very red and he was chewing tobacco.

He looked at Elf, then at Susan. "Ladies," he said, touching the bill of his baseball cap. The smell of sweat and whiskey came off him in a palpable mist. But he moved on his massive legs as steadily and smoothly as a ballet dancer.

Duffy again felt he had to introduce himself, since it looked like nobody else was going to. He held out his hand. "Sir," he said. And when the big man swung his huge bony head to look at him: "My name's Duffy Deeter. This is Susan Gender. We here for the hunt. Come up from Florida."

"You in good company, Duffy Deeter." He took his hand. "Miss Susan, my pleasure." He put his arms around Willard and Joe Lon. "These'er my boys here. Finest damn boys I ever coached. Good men on and off the field. Coach Tump Walker's my name. I got boys all over this country. Playing on six pro teams, coaching two. You met Buddy Matlow since you been here?"

"No, I don't believe I've had the pleasure."

"Damn right," said Coach Tump. "Well, he's one of mine too. All I got's my boys. I don't like to brag. I *don't* brag." His face got redder as he talked. "Ever goddam one of'm eat bullets. One of my boys is George 'Big Freight' Lester!"

"Who?" said Duffy Deeter.

Coach Tump lifted one of his heavy legs and hustled his balls. "You don't know who Big Freight Lester is?"

"Don't believe I do," said Duffy. He did, of course, know who he was but he didn't want to sound as though he followed football. Besides, he was getting a tight feeling, claustrophobic, standing walled in on three sides by Willard and Joe Lon and their coach, and it was making him nervous. He always got mean when he got nervous.

"Big Freight ain't been nothing but all-pro ever year since he left Alabama is all he's been. He was one of mine too. Mean as a snake." He leaned down in Duffy's face, who didn't give an inch but pushed back and up with his own hard little face until their noses were practically touching. "Where'd you say you was from?"

"Florida," said Duffy.

"Went to Florida once," said Coach Tump. "Coaching clinic. Never went back, never expect to. Cain't trust any country where ever tree's got a light in it and a stick propping it up."

Willard put his hand on Duffy's shoulder. "He's all right, Coach. This'n right here is all right."

Coach Tump Walker hacked up a lunger, spit, and hustled his balls again. "He all right?"

"He *is* all right, Coach," said Willard.

He looked at Willard. "Boy, I want you to stay out of the bottle tonight." Then to the ladies: "You don't mind if a old man has a drink, do you? Chill's coming up now that good dark's here." He didn't wait for an answer, but reached a bottle from his baggy hip pocket and raised it. In the flashing light from the beauty contest stand where the musicians were sweating and screaming his thick throat pulsed in four quick, heavy spasms. He held the bottle out and looked at it. "It's one last drink in here, if anybody's . . ."

"Go on, Coach," said Joe Lon, "I got another one ain't been cracked in the pickup."

"It do help on a chilly night," said Coach Tump, finishing it.

Luther Peacock, Buddy Matlow's deputy, burst suddenly through the people packed together near the right side of the stage and came toward them. Even though the temperature had dropped ten degrees in the last few hours, Luther was sweating. His khaki shirt was sticking to the center of his chest.

"You got to do something," he said to nobody in particular, although he was looking at Susan Gender.

"What?" said Joe Lon.

"Where's the Sheriff?" Luther said. "Nobody seen Buddy?"

Willard belched and said, "I ain't been looking for him."

"Well, I have. I looked everwhere and he ain't nowhere." Luther stopped and looked into the crowd surrounding them on all sides as though he might see Buddy Matlow. "Sumpin's wrong," he said. "Sumpin bad's wrong."

"Buddy'll turn up," said Coach Tump.

"It's gone be trouble," said Luther Peacock. "I cain't handle it by myself."

"Handle what?" said Hard Candy.

"You ain't heard they turned two over?" said Luther.

"Turned two *what* over?" said Willard.

"Campers. It's just too many of'm here and it ain't enough water and it ain't enough room. They more fights this year than I ever seen before and now on top of it, Buddy Matlow's disappeared."

"Buddy ain't disappeared," said Joe Lon. "Most likely layin off in the bushes with somebody he's trapped."

Coach Tump said: "Don't talk like that about a teammate."

Just then there was a scream, a loud squealing scream over by the papier mâché snake that cut right through the music. They could see a tight little knot of people flying about over there, almost as if dancing, so rhythmic did the knot move. But they all knew they weren't dancing.

"Better go see what that is, Luther."

For the first time Luther seemed to calm down. Joe Lon

was one of the organizers of the Rattlesnake Roundup and Coach Tump was Honorary Chairman. If they were going to take all of it so lightly, Luther decided he would too. "I know what it is over there," he said, sucking his teeth reflectively, "and I ain't going near it."

Joe Lon took Elfie's arm and guided her a step or two away. He put the keys of the pickup in her hand. "Take these keys and git back to the trailer." She started to speak, but he shook his head. "I don't like all this. I never seen'm so rank."

Just as Elfie was leaving a tall, very thin man squeezed out of the crowd near the tree. He nearly cried he was so happy to see Coach Tump. He actually threw his skinny arms around Coach Tump's enormous shoulders and pressed himself against the straining mobile belly swinging under the coach's shirt. "Jesus, Jesus," he was saying.

Coach Tump turned his head off to the side and looked at Joe Lon. "This one's the one," said Coach Tump. "Tainted." Then he mouthed the word again: *tainted.*

The thin man seemed to see Luther Peacock for the first time. He turned loose Coach Tump, who had conspicuously kept his hands off him, enduring his embrace, and rushed over to Luther. He had to bend down to put his face in Luther's. "Sheriff, am I glad to see . . . am I . . ."

"Not the Sheriff," said Luther. "Deputy."

"They going nuts over by my camper. They . . ."

"Going nuts everwhere," said Luther, turning his hands up to examine his palms. Then he looked out over the crowd surging toward the stage where the band was beginning to falter. "I ain't responsible."

"They break open my camper, it's enough snakes in there to kill half of Georgia."

"I seen'm," said Coach Tump. "Sumbitch's got five hundred penned . . ."

"Cobras," the man said, "Russell's Viper, Mambas, Spotted rattlers, Mohave rattles, red diamonds, westerns . . ."

"Name Tommy Hugh," said Coach Tump. "He brought five hundred snakes *to* the Roundup."

"Tommy Hugh," said Tommy Hugh, shouting to make himself heard above the crowd. "I got pygmys and corals, an anaconda even. You got to do something."

"I believe, Gender," said Duffy Deeter, "Mystic, Georgia, has done tore its ass this time."

Willard Miller, his voice flat, laconic said: "It's blood in the air. I can smell it. I can *smell* the goddam blood in the air."

The band had quit now and the principal of the school was up on the stage trying to start the beauty contest. He was shouting into the microphone but every time he shouted the crowd roared back at him. He finally stopped, staring red-faced down into the surging men and women as he might have stared down at a crowd of unruly children in his auditorium. Except that his face was very red and he'd gone past just being scared. What showed in his eyes and on his trembling mouth looked like terror.

"What the hell we gone do?" said Joe Lon.

"We best go up there and git this straightened out," said Coach Tump, pulling his pants high onto his belly and then turning them loose and letting them slip again to the place where they rode low on his hips. Without waiting for an answer he charged toward the stage, his tackle-busting belly leading the way, knocking men, women, and children off their feet. When they got to the stage, he and Willard Miller and Duffy Deeter turned to face the crowd, while Joe Lon vaulted lightly up beside the principal and took the microphone. The principal smiled but he looked on the verge of tears. He shouted, "Joe Lon, you . . . you . . ."

Joe Lon put his mouth to the principal's ear: "Git over

there and line up the girls. The girls . . ." He shoved the principal toward the end of the stage, toward a low wall of plywood that formed an L-shaped room with no top where the girls stood pressed tightly together.

Joe Lon leaned in close to the microphone and said: "If you'd just quiet youself down," but he said it in a normal voice and even with the amplifier he couldn't hear his own voice. The most noise was coming from the place where the snake rose thirty feet in the air. The line of dancers circling the snake had torches now. It looked as though they had all found torches and they weren't so much singing, as they'd been doing before, but screaming. He stood watching, almost bemused by the whiskey running in his blood and the noise and the open fires. Then directly in front of him there was a high piercing cry like metal tearing, and when he looked down Joe Lon saw Duffy Deeter come straight up out of the crowd, lay out on the air as if he expected to do a half-gainer, but just as he was parallel to the ground the point of his heel caught a huge bearded man on the side of the head and his entire face splattered, some of the blood spotting the rough wooden boards of the stage. Willard Miller showing all his teeth in a great joyous scowl was on top of the man who had been kicked almost before he slipped to the ground.

Joe Lon waved to let the first girl come, and she did, wearing a bikini of some silver diaphanous material that had enough cloth in it to maybe make a glove. Her name was Novella and she was Hard Candy's chief rival for head cheerleader, although Novella was still in the tenth grade, but everybody knew—including Joe Lon, who was watching not her but the crowd's reaction to her—that it was only a matter of time before she took over from Hard Candy. She was favored tonight to take Miss Rattlesnake Queen and Joe Lon could tell by the way she pumped across the stage in her high-heeled shoes, all flashing legs and rounded arms over rounded breasts over rounded hips, her little matted, mounded beaver pulsing there where she kept her thighs peeled apart even as she pranced—Joe Lon could tell that she wasn't about to let a little thing like blood and fights keep her from what she'd been after since she was old enough to hold a baton.

There was still noise but it was all coming from seventy yards away where the torch-lit dancers tirelessly circled the snake. The audience spilled away from the front of the stage; everybody who could see her, had gone silent. Cigarette smoke and wood smoke hung in layers over their heads as they watched Novella move around the stage, giving them first a front view, then a side, then a back.

The principal had come back to the microphone and, reading from a little card, introduced Novella Watkins, gave her measurements, ". . . a fine young lady who will someday make somebody a fine wife at thirty-six, twenty, thirty-four . . . ," and her credits, ". . . Miss Junior Future Farmers of America, Miss Peach, Miss . . ." While he talked, Joe Lon eased to the end of the stage and dropped off into the dirt. He looked for Hard Candy and Susan Gender, but they were gone, along with most of the other women in the audience.

The snake was not supposed to be burned until after Miss Rattlesnake had been chosen. *She* was supposed to set the fire. But just as Joe Lon landed in the dirt at the end of the stage somebody touched the snake with a torch and the thing exploded into fire, lighting the entire football field like a bomb bursting. As if on signal, the solid wall of men collapsed in front of the stage, kicking and cursing and gouging. The contestants on the stage, startled by the explosion of fire, lock-stepped round and round in a sort of daze, all of them brilliantly lit by the burning snake.

Joe Lon could see plain enough that his old coach and

Willard and Duffy were in danger of being hurt bad. He deliberately turned and pushed his way out to the road. He picked his way through the parked cars and campers and finally turned into a dim woods road that would come out a quarter mile from his store. It felt good to be away from all those people, strangers and friends both. It felt good for the noise to diminish a little with each step that took him deeper in the woods.

When Joe Lon got to the store, Lummy was sitting on the stool behind the counter. He got off the stool when Joe Lon came in.

"How come it is folks hollering lak that?" said Lummy. A long sustained cheer floated back out of the pine trees. It might have been a football game they were hearing, except there were no rattles.

"How come it is?"

Joe Lon did not answer but only shrugged. Then: "George come in with that extra load of beer and whiskey?"

"He come in with that extree jus fine, Mr. Joe Lon."

Joe Lon hooked his heels on a rung of the stool, shivered, and hugged himself with his arms across his chest. "You feed the snakes?"

"Everone but the bettin snake."

"Feed him too," said Joe Lon. "And bring me out a bottle of that bonded."

Lummy went through the door into the little room at the back of the counter. He never picked up the rats with his hand. He wouldn't touch them. He wouldn't touch *anything* that was going to touch a snake, much less be *inside* a snake. He had a pair of long-handled needle-nosed pliers he used to lift the rats into the cages with the snakes. He used his pliers and did not wait to see the strike (he never did), but got the bottle of whiskey and took it to Joe Lon, where he sat waiting on a stool.

"How'd we do today?" he asked.

Lummy told him what they had sold, told him the store had done better than it had ever done at a Roundup. But Joe Lon didn't listen and Lummy knew he wasn't listening. But he went on explaining the little marks on his paper— how much beer, how much shine, how much bonded whiskey—just as he always did. He did what he was told to do, what it was his job to do, and he had absolutely no curiosity about why Mr. Joe Lon was mean tonight. He'd seen him mean often enough to know it when he saw it, but since he knew also that he had nothing to fear from Mr. Joe Lon, he didn't think about it.

His job was to be the nigger. That's the way he thought about it. *I am the nigger. That is the white man. There is a tree. There is a road. This is Mystic.*

That's the way it had to be as long as he was around a white man. As soon as he was *not* around a white man, he quit being a nigger and thought about many, many things that he did not ordinarily think about. One of the things he thought about was killing Mr. Joe Lon. Of course, as long as he was near him, he couldn't kill him, or even *think* about killing him. But when he was off by himself, or in the company of other black people, he not only thought about it, he often actually killed him.

Joe Lon turned his burned eyes on him. "Want a drink, Lummy?"

"Wouldn't mind a taste," Lummy said.

"Git youself a pint of that shine. No, shit, git a pint of that othern."

"Shine be good enough for ole Lummy."

"Git the othern, I said. You ain't got to mark it on you ticket."

"Go and git it," Lummy said to himself. "You ain't got to mark it on you ticket."

When he came back in Joe Lon was dialing the telephone. When he was through dialing it, he held it for a long time.

"Mayhap he out with them dogs," said Lummy licking the neck of the whiskey bottle.

Joe Lon said: "He ain't out with no dogs."

They both knew that the telephone was on a little wooden table beside the old man's bed. It sat on a metal dishpan turned upside down. Big Joe believed that when he couldn't hear it, he could feel it up on top of the metal pan vibrating. Said he could feel it right in the goddam air was what he said.

"It's me, Joe Lon," Joe Lon shouted into the telephone finally. *"Joe Lon!* How's Beeder?" A little spit flecked Joe Lon's lips and the lids of his ruined eyes seemed to work independently of one another. "I *know* I woke you up."

The old man claimed that his hearing was worse at night than in the day, and that it was the worst of all when he was just awakened. It took, he said, several hours for his tubes to clear out and drain good.

"How's Beeder?" he shouted again. And then, swinging to look at Lummy, "He says she's fine, just like she always is." He shouted back into the telephone: "Which is it? She fine? Or she like she always is?" He took a drink from his bottle, tilted on the stool, and winked at Lummy. He stiffened on the stool, a vein leapt in his thick neck. He screamed, "I don't know. Haven't seen a clock. Don't own a clock. Don't want a clock."

Lummy sat drinking his free bourbon in the corner, wondering how much of this he'd have to listen to before he could go home and get his woman and go for some of Junior's Real-Pit-Barbecue.

Joe Lon was screaming: "A family reunion! Right. All together again. I'll git Elf and the babies and you git Mama . . ." His voice was growing thicker and even though his face remained stunned and without expression, as though he might have been sleepwalking, tears came from his eyes and ran down over his heavy square chin, blue now with a stubble of beard. ". . . you git Mama and Beeder and I'll git Elf and the babies and you and me'll git'm all in a room in the big house and we'll just beat the shit out of them. Beat'm I said goddammit. Slap'm. Bust their faces."

He was crying openly now, his shoulders shaking, and Lummy, who recognized this as something he was not meant to watch, got up quietly and headed for the door, thinking only how grateful he would be for a good plate of Real-Pit-Barbecue and then his woman's warm thick back to sleep against. What was happening in there was none of his business.

Joe Lon was screaming: "We like that, don't we? Me and you? Hem'm up in a room and beat'm good?"

But Lummy might as well have been hearing a woodpecker in a tree or rain on a tin roof. It was the natural sound of the world, too much like everything else, and he wouldn't remember it.

The news that somebody had cut off Buddy Matlow's dick threatened to ruin everything: the dog fight that night and the snake hunt the next morning. It spread among the hunters and tourists like fire. Nobody had talked of anything else much all morning. It even served to take their minds off the fact that there was not enough water and the Johnny-on-the-spots were full to overflowing and several trailers had been wrecked the night before, two actually turned over.

Joe Lon found out about it when they woke him up shortly before noon. Coach Tump stood down in the yard hustling his balls and spitting tobacco juice into the dirt. He looked up at Joe Lon in the doorway to the double-wide and told him that Buddy Matlow had been taken to the hospital in Tifton, at least that is what most people were saying they'd heard, but there were others who said it was Macon where he'd been taken, and at least two or three said they'd heard that it was as far away as Atlanta.

Coach Tump said it didn't make much of a shit where they taken him if somebody'd gone and cut off his dick. "Wouldn't surprise me if this don't put a damper on the whole thing."

The story Coach Tump had heard said they'd packed it in ice. They had packed Buddy Matlow's dick in ice and salt and they meant to sew it back on and that was why they had gone all the way to Atlanta because they had better facilities for sewing dicks back on at the big hospital there.

"Damned if I'd want my dick sewed back on," said Willard Miller.

"I believe I would if they could do it like it was on there before," Coach Tump said.

Duffy Deeter said: "What goes around comes around." They had all come inside to drink coffee while Joe Lon got dressed. Duffy regarded his knuckles, all of them skinned and scabbed. He sucked gently at his nose. It was filled with black blood. "Bad karma," he said. "A guy that gets his dick cut off's got bad karma."

"He is also shit out of luck," said Willard Miller.

Joe Lon came out of the back, dressed now, his eyes webbed in a net of veins, his face puffy, and they all got in Coach Tump's Oldsmobile and drove out to Big Joe's to prepare Tuffy for the fight that night.

"Looks a little like war out there, don't it?" said Willard.

Joe Lon, who had been very quiet since they woke him up, only nodded. Out in the campground, a trailer was on its side. The road to Big Joe's was littered with cups and hotdog wrappers and hamburger wrappers and even articles of clothing. They passed four wrecked cars before they got to the schoolhouse.

"What the hell happened to you last night, boy?" said Coach Tump.

"I never known much about nothing oncet I got off that stage," Joe Lon said. "Them fuckers looked to eat me up."

"I'll drink to that," said Willard, running his thumbnail around the neck of a bottle of bourbon.

Coach Tump frowned. "Boy, I want you to stay out of the bottle today."

Willard said, "Coach, I just need a little something to smooth me out."

Coach Tump eyed the bottle. He would have beat hell out of any other boy playing for him if the boy had even *mentioned* drinking whiskey, much less doing it. But this was the Boss Snake of the team. He ran over anybody, everybody. As long as he did that, he could do whatever else he wanted to. "I guess a little whiskey won't hurt nothing."

They all had a little sip, except Joe Lon, who bubbled it pretty good. Willard Miller, who was sitting in the middle, reached over and hugged Duffy Deeter, then he kissed him on the cheek, right on top of a ragged purple bruise. "Joe Lon, damn if I don't think I'm in love with this little fucker right here. You see'm last night? Worsen a pit bull when you git'm down in the dirt."

"I was too busy tryin to not get eat myself to see anything," said Joe Lon.

While they drove on out to Big Joe's, they talked about last night, how they'd kicked and stomped and gouged and by God made sure Novella Watkins was crowned just like everbody known she ought to be.

The dogs that were going to fight that night, fifteen of them, had already been groomed and walked and were resting in their cages on the backs of pickup trucks when they got to the pit. The men who had brought them sat in the bleacher seats passing a sipping sack and spitting tobacco juice while they talked dog fighting. Joe Lon brought his daddy's Tuff out of the cage and took him into the pit to rub him down. It was the custom at Big Joe's to show the favorite in the pit while he was being groomed before the fight. Willard Miller and Coach Tump and Duffy went up into the bleachers while Joe Lon went for the dog. When he got back his daddy was up there too. All the faces of the dog fighters were turned toward Big Joe, who was talking.

Joe Lon knelt in the dirt beside the dog and smoothed him down with a heavy brush. The other dogs were making a terrible racket now that he had brought out Tuff. Joe Lon's head felt as if it might crack like bad glass and fall in pieces on the packed dirt where Tuff stood in his wide-legged stance, leaning slightly against the leash, his torn and scarred ears struck forward on his head. For a long time Joe Lon brushed and talked to Tuff in a soft, sympathetic whisper, telling him he was about to get to do what he had been bred and trained to do, that it wouldn't be long now before he could show everybody that he was the boss pit of all the bulls.

When he did look up for the first time, there in the bleachers on the opposite side from the dog fighters, sitting side by side, solemn and unsmiling, were Berenice and his wife, Elfie. He felt the sudden thrust of fear start in him. He couldn't think what they might be doing together. Elfie had been sullen and unusually quiet that morning. She'd hardly spoken to Coach Tump when he came into the trailer. Joe Lon didn't know what it was about and he didn't want to know. He didn't want anything except possibly to howl and he couldn't do that with everybody there watching.

Willard Miller came down out of the bleachers and sat on his heels on the edge of the pit. "Buddy Matlow ain't gitten his dick sewed back on; he's dead." He spoke in a hushed, careful voice. "Berenice's daddy says he was dead before they got to the hospital."

"Jesus," said Joe Lon. He felt a little sick to his stomach.

"The poor bastard did catch some shit in his life, didn't he."

"Nobody deserves to have his dick cut off. Listen, go up and bring the whiskey down here, would you?"

Willard got up and went into the bleachers. When he did, Elfie got up and came down to the pit. She didn't come into it but stood on the edge, watching him.

"What you and Berenice doing?" he said finally.

"She come by."

"What for?"

"Talk."

"Talk about what?"

"You."

"Me?"

"Us."

Joe Lon wished to God Willard Miller would come back and stop her talking to him. He raised his eyes to the bleachers and saw Willard standing up beside his daddy, looking down upon them but making no move to bring the whiskey.

"She told me what you said."

Joe Lon vigorously massaged Tuff's haunches.

"She said you said you loved her true. True love."

"Don't," said Joe Lon. "Christ, don't."

"Said you put it in her . . . and then stuck it in her . . . and then back again. Back again even after . . . after you . . . after the other."

He could only stare up at her dumbly.

"You never done that to me, Joe Lon, honey."

"No," he finally managed to say, "I never did."

"Does it mean you don't love me with true love?"

"No," he said. "For God's sake, Elf, git back up there and shut up about this. You don't know what the hell you're saying."

"I know what I know," she said. "After she told me I looked. She showed me and I looked. It's on the sheets. It's all over the sheets in my own bed, you and her and everthing."

"Elfie, goddammit, git away from me."

"Joe Lon, honey."

"What?"

"I cain't look at the babies any more. I tried this morning after she showed me and I cain't look at the babies any more. I'm too shamed. You shamed me so I cain't look at my own babies."

She turned and went back up the bleachers. Joe Lon called to Willard Miller and he started down the bleachers but then stopped. Joe Lon followed his gaze to the place Willard was looking and Berenice had started down the bleachers toward him.

Christ, they were taking turns. They were all going to take a turn at him. "You gone bring me the goddam drink, or what?" he shouted up at Willard Miller. But Willard didn't move.

The first thing Berenice said was, "She knows."

"Berenice," he said. "I may have to kill you."

"I made a clean breast of it," she said.

Joe Lon savagely massaged Tuffy's broad, muscled chest.

"I told everybody. I even told Shep. It was something about poor Buddy getting his . . . that happening . . . the way it did and all. His blood is all over the living room. I couldn't stand it. So I told just everybody. Shep said he understood and he'd always love me."

"Love you," he said.

She turned and went back up the bleachers. He watched her go and saw that Shep was sitting with Elfie now, talking earnestly, head to head.

Willard came down with the whiskey. "What'as you waiting for?" demanded Joe Lon.

"I didn't think I ought to break in on that. What was it they'as saying to you anyway?"

"Nothing."

"Well, here comes the fucker from the debate team to give you some more nothing." Willard turned and went back up the bleachers to where the dog fighters had just cracked another bottle.

Sure enough, Shep was coming down into the pit with him. Joe Lon didn't think he could stand it. There was a sudden blood lust on him. He was afraid he might fall upon Shep and tear his throat out.

"I come to tell you about Sheriff Matlow," Shep said.

Joe Lon opened his mouth to say he didn't want to know anything, that he couldn't stand to have anything else told to him by anybody. But instead of speaking he simply croaked, a hoarse, cracked noise deep in his throat. He opened the whiskey Willard had brought down and took a drink.

"Listen," said Shep in a shy, deeply embarrassed voice, "I know about you and Berenice. About how you were lovers. How in love you both were a long time ago here in Mystic. Love . . . Well, love . . . And then yesterday at your house . . ."

Joe Lon stood up and stretched his neck to breathe. He felt as though he had his head in a sack of cotton. The dog fighters had moved down a little closer to the pit. They sat now in the second row. They stared intently at his daddy's Tuffy, who had not barked or even growled but still stood with his dark ears forward on his head, leaning in the direction of the other penned bulls where they barked and growled and howled in their cages.

"Walk him around, boy," called Big Joe. "Take him around the pit."

Joe Lon led Tuff through a tight little circle around and around the pit. They were betting up there, making the bets that would stand tonight between the owners. Shep had never stopped talking, saying he understood. Berenice had told him everything and he understood everything. Joe Lon wanted to tell him that he didn't understand anything but he didn't trust himself to try to speak.

Shep followed him around the pit, close at his shoulder on the opposite side from Tuff. ". . . and he actually handed me his . . . his penis. Put it right in my hand and the blood was everywhere. It was cut off clean, I mean smooth at his belly and the blood was pouring out of the place where it was cut like it was a spigot. A blood spigot."

Joe Lon turned his pale, stricken face to Shep and managed to say: "Why you telling me this?"

"He said to," said Shep. "I thought I told you. He said to."

"Said to?"

"In the back seat, we got him in the back seat, and the doctor was driving and the last thing he said to me was, tell Joe Lon."

Joe Lon walked faster. The murmuring voices of the dog fighters floated into the pit over the constant barking of the caged bulls. More people had come into the bleachers now. High on the east side, Mother Well sat beside Victor, the snake preacher. As he watched, they both stood up and started down the bleachers seats toward him.

"Joe Lon," said Shep. "He said that. That's what Sheriff Matlow said. He said: Tell Joe Lon. But . . ."

Victor, the tight tufts of twisted hair shining in the weak sunlight like screws driven into his skull, was coming directly toward him, and Mother Well was a step behind him. Joe Lon had stopped. They were staring right into his eyes and he couldn't look away.

". . . but I think he was trying to tell me something else. I mean I think Sheriff Matlow wanted me to tell you some *thing*. That's the way it sounded. Tell Joe Lon . . . Then he died. Just quit breathing."

Joe Lon stood in the pit and watched Victor and Mother Well come right up to the barrier and stop. Everything seemed to move at three quarter time and there was about it the quality of a nightmare. Mother Well had a handful of snake rattles. She rolled them through her fingers like beads. Joe Lon could see each of them separate and distinct as they moved against the marble-smooth skin of her hands.

Victor raised his arms and his voice boomed into the pit: "I heard Jehovah speak terrific from his holy place and saw the words of the mutual covenants divine chariots of gold and jewels with living creatures starry and flaming with every color lion tiger horse elephant eagle dove fly worm and the wondrous *serpent* . . ."

Joe Lon started to howl. He let his head drop back on his shoulders and howled directly into the blue sunless sky.

". . . clothed in gems and rich array human in the forgiveness of sins according the covenant Jehovah."

Joe Lon didn't stop howling and Willard Miller came over the barrier with a forearm flipper that struck Shep such a lick it carried him all the way out of the pit.

Big Joe and the other dog owners were on their feet and Big Joe was calling to Joe Lon not to go crazy like his sister did. "Don't go crazy, Joe Lon! Don't go crazy!"

Victor was still booming away above him there, saying now: "I want you snakes! I want *all* you snakes!" And the dogs had been so stirred up by all the howling and hollering they were going crazy in their cages. Even Tuffy was howling, his head back, looking into the same blue empty piece of sky with Joe Lon.

Joe Lon fainted, or passed out, or maybe he went crazy there for a while because when he woke up he was in a dark room in his daddy's house. Elfie was there and so was Willard. Joe Lon first heard Beeder's television on the other side of the wall and beyond that the slashing, abrupt sound of dogs fighting and over the sound of the dogs the awesome roar of people screaming.

"You awake, Joe Lon, honey?" He didn't answer but let his eyes swing to Willard, where he stood on the other side of the bed. "You know what I said, Joe Lon, honey? Member? I didn't mean that. Don't you worry a minute. You hear? I love . . ."

"What time is it?" asked Joe Lon.

"Damned if you didn't go down for the count, Biggun," said Willard Miller.

"What time is it?" His head was splitting and his tongue felt swollen.

"It ain't midnight yet. Ain't far away though."

"Midnight? It cain't be."

"We got over to Doctor Sweet's, he given you a shot. He said it was most likely Buddy and everything caused you to do it. Jesus, it was a mess, too. I went over there and seen the car they hauled Buddy in. Looked like somebody'd butchered a hog in it."

"They know who killed him?"

"No, and I don't look for them ever to find out either. Weren't but several hundred had reason to cut his dick off."

"Who's with the babies?"

"Sarah's sleeping over. They fine, Joe Lon, honey."

"How come I'm here? Why ain't I home?"

Elfie opened her mouth to speak, then shut it and looked at Willard.

Willard said: "I think everbody's afraid you'd go nuts over there and . . . Shit, I don't know what you mighta done. What the hell *did* go wrong with you anyhow?"

"I don't know," he said. And he didn't. But he knew he'd been scared there in the pit as he'd never been scared before. And it was not any one thing that scared him. It was everything. It was his life. His life terrified him. He didn't see how he was going to get through the rest of it. He was miserable beyond measure. Everything seemed to be coming apart. He could see the frayed and ragged seams of everything slowly unraveling.

"Fuck it," said Willard. "It don't matter. Anybody's subject to go a little nuts now and then." Willard snorted an ugly little laugh through his nose. "I think I about broke three of the debate player's ribs for him."

"You probably shouldn't a done that."

"Nobody blamed me for it. You was hollering and he was the closest to you. I didn't know what was happening. I hit the first thing I could see. It happened to be the debate player."

"What ailed that goddam preacher?"

"Nothing. Shit, he was just putting in his order for you snakes. He wanted to buy'm that's all. You didn't burn a fuse over that, did you?"

"I don't want to talk about it any more."

"Good," said Willard. "It's beginning to bore the shit out of me, too. Next time you go nuts, I'd be obliged if you'd do it when I'm not around. You bout tore my goddam ear off."

Joe Lon sat up on the side of the bed. He remembered it

all now, the old man shouting about snakes, everybody coming to him in the pit, barking and barking at him, and the overwhelming feeling that he was going to be in there the rest of his life with everybody he'd ever known filing past to tell him how he'd failed. When he'd got started howling, Coach Tump and Duffy and Willard and his daddy had all fell on him and thrown him in the back seat of the Coach's old Oldsmobile with his daddy screaming for him not to go crazy. He even remembered taking hold of Willard's ear and refusing to let go on the ride to Doctor Sweet's.

"Shit," said Joe Lon. "You should a goddammit let me alone."

One final ragged cheer went up from the dog fight behind the house and then there was silence except for the steady drone of the television on the other side of the wall.

"I got to get Tuffy and go," said Willard. "It's his up."

"I'm coming," said Joe Lon.

"Hon, do you think you ought to go out there?"

"Where's my goddam shirt?"

"Coach Tump said he'd handle the dog with me." Willard gave Joe Lon his quiet, savage smile. "You going semi-nuts and all."

Tuffy was kept in a dark cool cage in the old man's room for the final hours just before a fight. Joe Lon spoke to him while Willard leashed him. Tuffy stretched, yawned, shook himself, and then seemed to hear the noise of the crowd outside for the first time. The short wiry hair rose on his shoulders, his ears got up, and a little slobber slipped spinning from his mouth. They led him down the hall to the back door and then through the dark to the ring of light where the bleachers and the aisles and all the open spaces under the bleachers were packed with men, women, and children. Their faces under the lights looked flushed and damp even though it was nearly forty degrees. Novella Watkins, wearing her little gold-gilt crown of snakes, sat in her place of honor at the head of the pit as was the custom after the beauty contest. Her daddy, a pig farmer, sat on one side of her and Slimey, one of the leaders in the rock band, sat on the other. Slimey still had on his sequined suit. A space opened up for Willard, joined now by Coach Tump, to get through to the pit. Joe Lon went to sit with his daddy just behind the barrier on the right side, not because he particularly wanted to sit with him but because his daddy kept a place there for himself and his friends and it was the only spot left to sit down.

His daddy glanced at him briefly. "How you feeling?"

"I'm all right."

"You feeling all right?"

"I told you."

"I thought you'd gone crazy shore." He spit a long stream of tobacco juice and passed Joe Lon the bottle he was sipping from. "What the hell ails you, anyway?"

Joe Lon sat, refusing to answer.

"It's just Buddy's dick cut off got you upset. Enough to upset anybody. Hope they catch the sumbitch done it. But they won't. Never do. Anybody worth a shit gits killed, they never find out who done it." He leaned forward and looked around his son. "Evening, Elf. Things been lively, ain't they?" Without waiting for an answer, he looked back to his son. "You got anything on the fight?"

"I got a dollar or two down."

"I hope you didn't give no odds. Tuffy's got all he can handle with this sumbitch."

"I don't give odds on nothing," said Joe Lon.

The other dog had been brought into the pit. He was straining and slobbering and snapping before he ever got onto the sand, bloodied now from earlier fights. His name was Devil and everybody there who had the slightest interest in dog fighting knew him. He carried more scar tissue than even Tuffy did.

This particular fight was Louisiana rules, which meant that a dog didn't have to die. There was nothing compulsory about one dog taking a killing, although he could take his killing if he wanted to. Any dog that would face could fight. If he wouldn't face, he was retired from the pit and the other dog was declared the winner.

Only one handler for each dog was allowed in the pit. Willard came down with Tuffy. Coach Tump stayed directly behind him outside the pit. The coach handed Willard a towel and a bowl of water. That was all each handler was allowed to bring into the pit. If it had been hot weather, he would have been allowed a fan to cool the animal down with at pickups. The dogs, held on opposite sides of the pit by heavy leashes, were allowed to slowly come together on the hard, packed earth until their foreshortened blunt heads were only inches apart. They were both straining, their eyes shot with blood, their nostrils flared, in an utter frenzy. Most of the crowd was standing, shouting bets at one another and screaming at the dogs. Novella Watkins was hollering her little heart out, stamping her feet and shaking her dainty fist, but even in her excitement, one of her hands kept returning to her head to check her tiny crown of snakes. Joe Lon saw Duffy Deeter across the pit in the stands. Hard Candy and Susan Gender were with him. The old man they'd kicked around at the bar, Poncy, sat between the two girls. They all looked a little out of control, except Poncy, who sat quietly staring at the ends of his fingers. Down in the pit, the referee stepped onto the sand. He was an old man, a tobacco farmer from Tifton. He was wearing brand-new overalls and a black felt hat. He glanced up at Big Joe, who nodded, and then across to the man from east Tennessee.

He looked to the handlers and said, "Are we ready to let'm roll, gentlemen?" They both nodded. The referee's call had a high joyous lilt: "Let'm roll!"

The handlers slipped the leashes and the dogs met in the center of the pit. The impact as they came together had the sound of an ax in wood, a deep solid joining. It was impossible to follow what was happening as they rolled in the dirt, but when at last they stopped, Tuffy had been cut along the back and across the top of the skull. But it was Devil who was caught. Tuffy had managed to close on the side of his neck, not far enough under to get the jugular, but it was a mean, wearing hold. He closed his eyes and rode the other dog down. Devil was strong enough to regain his feet at times and lift Tuffy nearly clear of the ground but he couldn't shake him and eventually they were in the dirt again.

They lay there for two or three minutes and then Tuffy shook Devil so hard that he shook himself loose from the hold and went flying across the pit. They both scratched in the dirt in an effort to join again, and when their roll stopped Devil was into Tuffy's belly and Tuffy was into Devil's haunch. They shook each other where they lay. Both dogs were slick with blood, but neither was pumping. As long as they didn't hit an artery or a heavy vein, the blood didn't really matter. The dogs never seemed to notice it. When the referee called for the first pickup forty minutes later, it was not at all clear which was the better dog. The dogs' jaws had to be pried open with a hickory wedge before they could be handled.

Willard Miller took Tuffy, who was so fiercely mad his

eyes were crossed, to the bowl, gave him some water, and washed the blood out of his nose; then he put each of the dog's feet into the bowl.

The referee said: "Are you ready to let'm roll, gentlemen?" And the two dogs were back in the dirt again.

The second pickup was not until an hour later and it had been a brutal standoff match. Bets had been made and re-made and made yet again. There had been several fights in the stands. One had been going on for the last twenty minutes and had worked its way around to the side of the pit. Bets were starting to be laid off on the two men rolling around in the dirt while the dogs were being handled.

"He's pumping," Willard said to Coach Tump. Tuffy's rear right leg was pumping blood. He turned and looked over to Big Joe, whose face was passive. He nodded. Let'm fight.

But this time when the referee called to let'm roll, and the heavy leashes were slipped, Tuffy turned. He'd lost a lot of blood and it was still spurting from his back leg. He staggered as the other dog came across the ring. The referee called for a pickup. Devil's jaws were pried out of Tuffy's back. The referee was not sure of the move Tuffy had made, whether he had truly refused to face or not. The crowd was going crazy and their stamping feet on the boards of the bleachers rolled over the pit like thunder. The fight between the two men was over. One of them lay face down in the dirt. The other man hung over the wall watching the bleeding dogs.

When the referee had them face again, there was no doubt. Tuffy turned, but before the referee could declare the winner and have Tuffy withdrawn, Big Joe, the tails of his enormous black coat flapping behind him, had leaped over the barrier into the pit. He caught Tuffy against the boards. He and the crowd howled with a single voice while he kicked the dog to death.

Coach Tump sat red-eyed and hunkered over a yellow tablet of paper, a bitten nub of a pencil caught in his fingers. The little cheerleaders brought him steaming coffee in relays. It was very early but the snake teams were already forming up. Men, women, and children wandered about in front of the registration table where Coach Tump sat. It had been a wild calamitous night, with dancing and drinking and fighting and cars racing around over the countryside. Three more campers had been wrecked. Luther Peacock tried to do something about it all, even put two men in jail, but then he just gave up on it. There were too many people to try to do anything with.

Coach Tump stretched his neck, trying to see Joe Lon or Willard. He asked Hard Candy if she had seen them.

"Not this morning, Coach," she said, and gave him another cup of coffee. He laced this cup heavy with whiskey. It made him feel a little better. Fog lay curling among the far trees. The heavy pine smell of sap rising was everywhere on the air. It was damp and had grown colder during the night. A great day for hunting snakes. They'd all be in the ground. Coach Tump wished to God it was all over. The last thing in the world he wanted to do was sit here and register snake-hunting teams. But they'd gone too far with it to stop now. He'd talked with Willard and the doctor and Luther and even Big Joe—after Joe Lon had left in the truck with the bloody body of Tuffy thrown on the tailgate —Coach Tump had talked to them about the possibility of calling the hunt off. There seemed reason enough to do

it: Buddy's death, too many people, too little water, too few
toilets. But they had decided together that calling off the
hunt would probably drive the crowd over the final brink
to madness. They'd torn down most of the bleachers around
the pit while Big Joe was still kicking Tuffy, and they might
have torn down the house too if Joe Lon hadn't suddenly
come out the back door with his daddy's shotgun and let
off four rounds in the air. The shotgun calmed them down
enough to get them off the place. But they were still dangerous and there was nothing to do but go on with the hunt.

A man suddenly came running out of the woods, screaming, the fog swirling at his pumping knees. He was running
and screaming and Coach Tump recognized him as the one
who was tainted from keeping over five hundred snakes on
his personal property.

"They killing him. *Killing!* Butchering . . . My friend. Oh,
Jesus God, my *only* friend."

Coach Tump got him calmed down, but never enough
to find out exactly what was happening, only that somebody
was getting killed. Since Buddy was dead and since Luther
Peacock was nowhere about and since he, Coach Tump, *was*
Honorary Chairman of the Roundup, he ran across the
campground with Tommy Hugh and found five men, a
woman, and two small children attacking a snake, a con-
strictor, eighteen feet long and more than two hundred
pounds. The snake did not move; it didn't even look alive.

Tommy Hugh was screaming that it was hurt already from
the cold, that it had no place to hide last night and its body
temperature was down in the forties, and that besides it was
harmless. Harmless! But the men and women were screaming about skin and food and steaks and danger. Danger!
And they were hitting the snake with hatchets. They all had
hatchets. Even the children. The snake did writhe some be-

fore they got its back open, but not much and it didn't last long.

Finally, all of them, even the children, were standing in the snake. There was an enormous amount of guts and blood and it didn't smell good at all. The men and women got out of the snake and made the children get out of it and they stood for a moment regarding the two-hundred-pound mess of stinking guts and blood and mutilated skin and without saying anything walked out from under the trees where they found the snake. They stopped once to chop their hatchets into the dirt to clean off the blood and bits of whitish meat, but they never looked back.

Tommy Hugh actually knelt and lifted the anaconda's head into his lap. The head had fared better than the rest of the snake. It only had two parallel hatchet marks in the skull between the eyes.

Tommy Hugh looked up at Coach Tump, tears streaming down his face, and said: "You would've stopped them if it'd been a dog they was chopping."

Coach Tump stood for a moment and then said before he turned to go: "You tainted sumbitch."

The coach walked back to the table, his stomach a little sick, and feeling very bad about the morning. Luther Peacock was there, with a cup of coffee, and Joe Lon was sitting in his pickup truck beside Willard. Duffy Deeter was leaning on the fender. Big Joe's shotgun, the one Joe Lon had fired the evening before, was on a rack behind Willard's head. The tailgate of the pickup was still down. Coach Tump came up to the table and took a mean swallow of his whiskeyed coffee and told them about the tainted sumbitch with the two-hundred-pound snake.

Joe Lon did not answer but sat regarding the far wall of dark pine where it started to rise to the scrub oak ridge

above which the sun was a thin white disk in the cold fog
rising out of the ground. That long oak ridge above the
pines was where they would hunt the snakes. He'd taken
Tuffy off last night behind the field to an old storm-blasted
pine tree where the buzzards roosted and pulled him off the
tailgate. Joe Lon watched him for a long moment lying there
with the blood still damp on his scarred body; then he'd
driven home and had the first real night's sleep in months.
He had put himself carefully on the bed beside Elfie and
carefully closed his eyes and listened to his heart beating.
Elfie had taken his hand and he let her hold it. She lay very
still on the bed. Finally she said: "Goodnight, Joe Lon,
honey."

"Goodnight," he said.

"Things'll be different tomorrow," she said.

"All right," he said.

Then he had gone carefully to sleep, a deep dreamless
sleep, because he knew and accepted for the first time that
things would not be different tomorrow. Or ever. Things got
different for some people. But for some they did not. There
were a lot of things you could do though. One of them was
to go nuts trying to pretend things would someday be different. That was one of the things he did not intend to do.

"We gone have to git'm started," said Coach Tump.
"They nervous and ready to go."

"We might as well," said Luther Peacock.

There were three people on a team. Sometimes a man, his
wife, and their child. Sometimes two men and a woman.
Sometimes three men. One carried the stick, one the hose,
and one the little bottle of gasoline. Coach Tump Walker's
pad showed that there were seventy-five officially registered
teams, but a lot of people hadn't bothered with signing up,
because it was obvious that better than six hundred people
—laughing, shouting, drinking, cursing—were strung out

waiting for the race up the hill.

Luther Peacock got in the cab of the pickup beside Joe Lon. "Let's go, boy," he said.

They started them this way every year. Coach Tump and some of his boys—in this case, Willard Miller and Duffy Deeter—would stay down with the hunters, making sure they kept lined up and there were no false starts, while Joe Lon and Buddy Matlow (today Luther Peacock) would drive the pickup through the border of rising pines on a little dim road that finally rose to the sandy ridge of scrub oaks and palmetto. Joe Lon drove carefully, his eyes straight ahead, grunting now and again when Luther Peacock spoke to him. It was only about four hundred yards up through the pines to the long, slightly curving oak ridge where hundreds and hundreds of gophers had burrowed long slanting holes into the sand. That was where the rattlesnakes lived, in the gopher holes, never molesting their hard-shelled, lethargic hosts, but seeking shelter there in the warm holes when cold weather came. The snakes' cold blood could not bear winter. If the temperature dropped below thirty-two degrees, they simply froze solid on the spot unless they could get themselves underground.

Joe Lon and Luther got out of the pickup and walked over the crest of the ridge. A chicken wire and plywood snake pen identical to the one in the school yard had been set up to receive the snakes. A pair of scales hung by the pen. Little blue tags that would register the weight and length of each snake sat waiting on the scales. The starting seniors on the Mystic Rattlers football team would weigh and measure the snakes. The cheerleaders, led by Novella Watkins, would record weight and length on the blue tags for the hunters.

"Wait," said Joe Lon. "Wait a minute."

Luther Peacock had taken out his red handkerchief.

"We got to do it," said Luther.

From this high ridge of ground, Joe Lon could see the whole thing. Over there to the left was the campground and beyond it, his trailer, where Elfie was probably washing and feeding the babies. The senior football players were already bringing the cheerleaders up through the pine trees, getting a head start on the hunters, who always went a little berserk when the signal to start was given. Straight ahead and perhaps three hundred yards behind the cheerleaders, whose bright little uniforms flared like something growing in the dark woods, stood the hunters, their solid straining faces turned up watching for the signal. And on the farthest horizon, Joe Lon could see the hazy outline of his daddy's twin-gabled roof. He wondered if Beeder would be watching. She said she would be watching, that she always watched the howling ascent of the hunters to the traditional snake ground of the Mystic Rattlesnake Roundup.

"We got to do it," said Luther.

"Yeah," said Joe Lon. "I guess we got to."

Luther Peacock raised his red handkerchief over his head, and when he did the line of hunters broke, racing into the trees that led up to the oak ridge. The long snake sticks shook on the air like lances. A sustained squall of voices echoed out of the pine woods. As they watched, the senior football players and the cheerleaders sprinted out of the pine trees and started the last little climb up to the ridge.

Joe Lon went back to the pickup and opened the door. There was a bottle of whiskey in the glove compartment. He got into the cab and took it out. The sky had lowered since they had come up on the ridge. The weak sun could not burn off the fog still rising out of the ground. It was getting colder. Joe Lon strained to see the house below the twin gables on the far horizon. It was there. He could make it out but it was hazy. Beeder couldn't possibly see the hunters who were just now breaking onto the ridge and dropping to their knees by the gopher holes. Indifferently, he watched them scramble at the holes, pulling the sand away with their hands, clawing, setting it up for the hose. A strange peace, heavy, even tiring, had settled in him. He almost dozed as he watched them, frantic, jerking and howling, every one of them intent on being the first to pull a snake out of the ground. He sipped the whiskey and wondered what it would be like over there where Beeder was. The hunters must look smaller than ants. Maybe they couldn't even be seen. He thought they couldn't. She had said otherwise.

"Oh, I can see them," she said. "I can see just as much of them over there as I want to see."

He'd just come back in the house with the shotgun. Outside trucks were starting up. Now and then dogs started barking.

"I've seen more of them than I want to see," he said. "I wish we didn't have to do this. I wish I'd never heard of a rattlesnake."

"Daddy would say to wish in one hand and shit in the other, see which one fills up first."

He said: "I know what daddy would say." He turned toward the door. "I got to go."

"What you gone do with him?"

"Take him out yonder where the buzzards roost."

"Okay," she said.

"I don't think Tuffy felt anything much. He was already hurt pretty bad."

"It don't matter," she said.

"No, I don't reckon it does."

Somebody had brought up some lightered knots and made a fire behind the snake pit. The black pine smoke rose with the fog into the lowering sky. Snakes were already being put into the pit. All across the barren ridge, the hunters stood in dark relief against the winter sky, pulling the snakes from the ground, stretching them at the ends of the long poles. Somebody had let Poncy on a team. He handled the gasoline. Joe Lon, sitting utterly still in the truck listening to his heart beat between sips of whiskey, watched as the team Poncy was on dropped by a fresh gopher hole. One man ran a ten-foot length of garden hose down the hole until he was sure it was all the way to the bottom. Then Poncy measured out a teaspoon of gasoline and poured it down the hose. If there was a snake in there, he'd be up in a minute, drunk and blinking from the gas fumes. Poncy and the two other hunters stepped back from the hole and waited. Presently, the blunt dry head of the snake appeared, the black forked tongue waving, testing the air. There was a smooth undulation and another foot of snake, thick as a man's wrist, appeared. One of the hunters dropped the noose at the end of the stick over the snake's head and pulled it tight. Slowly, a five-foot length of serpent was drawn out of the hole. Poncy was dancing around, making the wild excited cries a child might make.

"Hold him, hold him," Poncy was begging. The man held the writhing snake up on the end of the stick. Poncy came closer and closer until he was looking right into the snake's eyes. Poncy hissed. From less than a foot away, he shot spit into the snake's gaping, fanged mouth. Just as he was about to do it again, he looked up and saw Joe Lon watching him. Almost shyly, he averted his eyes. But while the man with the stick took the snake to the pit, Poncy came over to the truck where Joe Lon was sitting with the door open. He was flushed, smiling, his eyes bright.

"Hi," Poncy said.

Joe Lon took another careful sip of whiskey and did not speak. Poncy looked embarrassed. "I don't care what you did in the bar," he said. Joe Lon wanted to say something so the old man would go back and start pulling snakes out of the ground and leave him alone. But he didn't think he could speak. So he carefully nodded his head. Poncy seemed to accept that as an answer.

Poncy leaned closer and for the first time held Joe Lon's eyes. He said: "I know why you did it. It's natural, and I don't hold it against you."

Joe Lon nodded. Poncy turned and started back to his team but he stopped and looked at Joe Lon before he'd gone very far. "I'd rather be here on this hill with these snakes and you," he said, "than anywhere else in the world."

Willard Miller, Duffy Deeter, and Coach Tump walked out of the pine trees and Joe Lon watched while they came up the crest of the hill to the truck. When they stopped by the open door, Joe Lon handed Coach Tump the whiskey bottle because he was afraid the coach was going to speak to him and Joe Lon was no longer sure that he could answer. But not being sure he could speak did not strike him as odd. It seemed normal enough, even good. They passed the bottle. The temperature had dropped twenty degrees since daylight. A light inconstant buzz of rattles floated out of the pit and hovered over the hill.

Luther Peacock, leaning against the fender of the truck, said in a quiet voice: "You know I never touched a goddam snake in my life. Sumbitch if I know how they do that." Everywhere in front of them, the dark silhouettes of men were joined to the earth by the thick stretched bodies of snakes. The sky gave no light at all now except where the thin white disk of sun hung in the east.

Off and on all morning, Victor, his hair more wildly twisted than ever, appeared among the hunters, to urge them on to greater efforts. So Joe Lon was not surprised to see him come out from behind the snake pit. But he was surprised to see him suddenly stop and strip to the waist. The men and women nearest Victor turned just in time to see Victor bend to his heavy coat lying on the ground and open the pockets. When he straightened up he had a rattle-snake in each hand. He held the writhing snakes over his head. His voice boomed: "Ye shall take up . . ."

A rush of energy shocked through Joe Lon. He stiffened on the seat. All morning he had felt as though he was going to do it today. But he had not known what *it* was. Now, watching Victor stagger across the crest of the ridge, Joe Lon knew what it was he had planned to do all along, the thing that had lain rank and fascinating in his brain since last night at the pit. He'd waited for the moment to come, the right one, knowing he'd recognize it when it did. The hunters were scattering in front of Victor, his heavy lilting voice singing on about good and evil in a kind of mad howl. When the old man finally stepped between Joe Lon and the fog-shrouded, twin-gabled house on the far horizon, Joe Lon reached to the rack where the shotgun hung behind him and in a single movement came out of the cab and blew a hole the size of a doorknob out of Victor's pale naked chest.

The hunters who had been scattering stopped. Nothing moved anywhere. Joe Lon jacked another round of double-ought buckshot into the twelve-gauge pump, let the gun drop slightly to the right, and blew the look of horror right off Luther Peacock's head. A woman's voice said a word, begging. A child cried. And Joe Lon strolled casually toward the hunters, pumping the shotgun. When he threw it to his shoulder, the bead swung right past Shep and held on Berenice. He shot away her neck. Joe Lon jacked in another shell. He felt better than he had ever felt in his life. Christ, it was good to be in control again. He shot the nearest hunter.

When he pumped the gun again, it was empty. Since the first shot, no more than seven or eight seconds had passed, during which time everybody on the hill stood in arrested motion. As he pulled down on the empty chamber for the second time, dozens of hunters scrambled for cover. But most of them did not. The man nearest him, his face twisted with fear and rage, screamed: "Git that crazy bastard!" And a whole wall of men and women, their mouths open, teeth bared, moved with a single raging voice upon Joe Lon. He never dropped the gun. He simply held it and waited as their hands came upon him and he was raised high in the air. The gun went into the snake pit with him. He fell into the boiling snakes, went under and came up, like a swimmer breaking water. For the briefest instant, he gained his feet. Snakes hung from his face.

As he was going down again, he saw, or thought he saw, his sister Beeder in her dirty white nightgown squatting off on the side of the hill with Lottie Mae, watching.

Harry Crews

Harry Crews was born and reared in Bacon County, Georgia. He teaches at the University of Florida in Gainesville, and is a contributing editor of *Southern* magazine. He is also a contributor to *Playboy, Esquire,* and many other magazines and newspapers. *A Feast of Snakes,* first published in 1976, was his eighth book.